from Slave to Soldier to Servant

WILLIAM FURMAN

Charleston, SC
www.PalmettoPublishing.com

from Slave to Soldier to Servant
Copyright © 2021 by William Furman

TXu 2-285-068

Hardcover ISBN: 978-1-68515-289-5
Paperback ISBN: 978-1-68515-290-1
eBook ISBN: 978-1-68515-291-8

Acknowledgments

A heartfelt thank you to each of the following:
Larry & Linda Bellville
Linda Bryant
Del Harris
David & Diana McKowen
Janet Wiggins
For your encouragement and assistance in the creation of this manuscript.

Foreword

This novel is based on actual people and events in history. However, it is not a historical manuscript. It is fiction. Therefore, the events presented here are not necessarily in historical accuracy nor in sequence. Also, some of the people in the story are not historically supported.

A first century glossary and a list of characters follow the story.

The original, accurate historical account of this story is provided following the list of characters.

Dedicated to my wife, Barbara, who brought my soul back to the Lord.

and to my brother

Chuck

Bill

I

The Birth of a Slave

During the reign of Emperor Augustus Caesar when Rome was at the height of its glory, a slave baby was born. Would this new child be allowed to live or would it be left on the side of a road to die? That was the custom if the baby was sickly or female. This child was a boy. That put him in the 'allowed to live' category. He was healthy; this also met the criteria for 'allowed to live'. Unfortunately, the mother died in giving birth to the child. That changed the decision-making process. The slave owner would decide the baby's fate.

The owner was a Roman Senator, Quintus Crassus, who had purchased the baby's father at Rome's monthly slave market five years before. The father was a Greek, named Fidelis Cornelius. It was rare that a slave with this man's qualifications was sold at the slave market. He had been owned by a man who had displeased Caesar, so everything the man owned, including Fidelis Cornelius, had been confiscated and was to be auctioned off rather than being processed through a private sale.

The Senator had been in a position to hear of this sale beforehand and was told of the slave's intellectual background. He was particularly interested since he was searching for a tutor for his son and two daughters. Senator Crassus made certain he would be at the market on the day of the sale, and he successfully outbid the other potential buyers. Fidelis turned out to be an excellent tutor. The children loved him and the parents developed a fondness for him.

Fidelis was allowed to come and go as he pleased. As time went on, he was allowed to take a wife, who was also a slave. He was given permission to build his own house, so this family's home was a much more solid structure than the usual home (called "insulaes") of the lower class of people. Fidelis and his wife were soon parents of a baby girl they named Livia. Five years later his wife died giving birth to their second child, a baby boy.

Fidelis was devastated when his wife died giving birth to the baby. His mourning was so noticeable that Senator Crassus, being a compassionate person, was also saddened by her death. He allowed the baby to live, thinking it might be a comfort to Fidelis. To provide for the baby he made arrangements for another female slave to nurse and care for the baby until he was weaned. The baby was named Titus Cornelius.

The baby was weaned about the time Livia turned eight. She became a mother to Titus as well as the cook and the housekeeper for the family. As Titus grew, his family lived in the small home that his father had built, single-handedly. It was not as cramped and smelly as the insulaes that most of the slaves and lower classes lived in. Not only were their homes unsound structures, they were fire hazards. The Cornelius family felt fortunate to live where they did.

All slaves had an assignment they were expected to fulfill which varied from slave to slave. For the Cornelius family, a typical day would include Fidelis spending most of the day tutoring the Senator's children on Greek, mathematics, poetry, reading and some knowledge of science. While their father was tutoring, Livia and Titus were assigned household chores at the domus.

Fidelis' teaching efforts provided the senator's children a better education than many other Roman children received. Each day, Fidelis would take the children out into a field or have them sit under a tree to recite what they had learned the day before. Then he would introduce a new subject or a concept. If it rained or was cold, they would remain under roof in the courtyard; only as a last resort would they stay inside. Because of the open setting Fidelis used to teach the Senator's children, Livia and Titus were able to attend the daily lessons and receive the benefit of his teaching. However, they had daily choirs that had to be completed before they were able to take advantage of this opportunity.

Fidelis taught for 14 years. During this time a deep, loving and caring relationship grew between the tutor and his students despite the difference in their social class. These feelings never diminished and actually increased as the years passed. But the fact was, Fidelis and his children were slaves. They were told where they would live and what they were to do. Their future would always be in the hands of their owner.

Even though the Cornelius family was in the lowest level of society, they accepted their status without any question. They had always been treated well by the Senator's family, which gave Fidelis and his children a sense of loyalty and a feeling of security.

Although none of the family tasted the whip or was abused in any way, they still were slaves and did not have the right to utilize any of the privileges of Roman citizenship, such as using the public baths, which was a very important privilege to a Roman. It was at the baths that men would mix freely with their fellow citizens, bathing and conversing. No other culture had public baths and to the Romans, this placed their culture above all others. The baths made them feel superior to rest of the world.

There were only two categories of people in Roman culture, citizens and non-citizens. Those who were citizens included wealthy people, artisans, some shopkeepers, and others all the way down to the legionaries in the army. They enjoyed privileges that were denied the non-citizens.

The highest level in Roman culture were the wealthy. For them life was good. Most lived on the hills outside of the city of Rome in large homes called a domus that were built around an unroofed courtyard. The rooms of these homes reflected the wealth of the family. The wealthier the family, the more elaborate the furnishings. The owners were surrounded by servants and slaves that cared and provided for them. A few, usually those classified as Senators, maintained two homes, one outside of the city, in the clean air free of city odors, the other inside the city for use when the affairs of government required their presence.

The non-citizen category consisted of foreigners, freed slaves and slaves. The free non-citizen people lived behind or above the shops, where they worked. This was usually in a two-room home. A few of the non-citizens became shop owners but still lived above their shop. The slaves and poor lived in shabbily built insulaes that were fire traps or subject to collapsing.

All Romans, no matter what class they belonged to, shared a few traditions; one such tradition was the worship of Jupiter, Minerva and other common gods. Their worship was thought to be the means by which they could merit the blessings of the gods and thereby gain prosperity for themselves. Another tradition they shared revolved around mealtime rituals. Breakfast and lunch were light meals often eaten with friends or colleagues. The evening meal was a social event that was taken more seriously.

This was the environment in which Titus Cornelius grew from infant to teenager. He grew to a height of 1.75 meters tall and became quite muscular from doing field work rather than domestic work he had performed as a child. He had his father's Greek features of brown hair and dark eyes and his face was smooth.

The time finally came when the Senator's children reached adulthood and were no longer in need of a tutor. The Senator and his children gathered to discuss what to do with Fidelis and his children.

At first Senator Cassus felt Fidelis should be sold to another family that needed a tutor. But the Senator's children said," Fidelis has become part of our daily lives. It would not be the same if he were gone. Isn't there something else he could do for us here?"

The Senator asked, "Well, if you have any ideas, I'll consider it."

His son said, "The vineyard has been neglected for the last two years. Fidelis could make it productive again and his son could help him."

So Fidelis was put in charge of the family's vineyard rather than being sold to another family. And his teenage son, Titus Cornelius, had become a necessity as well according to the children. So, he was kept to assist in maintaining the vineyards. That left Livia. little thought was given to her. When Fidelis was told he and his son would be taking care of the vineyard but that Livia would be leaving, he asked the Senator to allow her to remain with him. The Senator just sighed and said, "Might as well keep the family together." She was allowed to stay.

Now, Fidelis, Titus and Livia felt secure in their new roles. A new day and a new relationship were dawning for Fidelis and his adult children. As father and son walked out into the fields the first day, Titus asked Fidelis, "Father, have you ever been responsible for a vineyard?"

"No, I have not, but I do know about plants and how to care for them."

"What about making wine?"

"I have never made wine before. We will be learning together. Hopefully, people will be patient with us."

The Senator was patient and the vineyard became prosperous, mostly because of Fidelis' knowledge and the physical labors of Titus.

One fall day as the leaves began to fall, Titus, standing on the brink of a hill, started looking out toward the horizon. He could see where the earth and the sky met. After viewing that scene for a moment, he slowly turned 360 degrees looking outward as far as he could. His father noticed Titus turning, and stopped picking grapes and watched him. Titus asked, "Does land go on forever?" Fidelis answered, "No, there are bodies of water called seas and oceans that separate land. Why do you ask?"

Titus said, "This land must be big and I have seen very little of **it.** It must be huge. Has it always been in existence, or did it have a beginning?"

"My, but you are asking deep questions and I'm not certain I can answer. I have always accepted the fact that the land was there and didn't think any more about it. I don't know if it had a beginning. But if it did, the gods had to be involved.

"I think it would take some great power to make this land. Father, are the gods that great?"

"Son, you are asking about things I have never learned about. To my knowledge, the gods have power to cause things to happen in their area of interest but that is all."

Titus started to ask another question but Fidelis cut him off by saying, "Right now we need to get these grapes picked."

Not long thereafter Senator Crassus died. Livia asked, "Father will this mean we could be sold?"

"I doubt it, Livia. We have always had a good relationship with the Senator's family. They didn't want us to leave when their father was alive and I don't think that has changed." Fidelis knew this was a real possibility, but he kept this concern to himself not wanting to worry his children.

Titus' sister Livia had always looked after him since he was a baby and into his teen years, even though she was five years older than he and considerably shorter. She had a maternal look about her. However now he no longer needed her guidance. As Titus matured, his strength increased and his skin darkened from working in the vineyards. He was content doing this type of labor and never gave any thought about being a slave. He had never experienced any other environment. Being something else never entered his mind even with the education he had received.

A surprise came when they found out that in the Senator's will, Fidelis was granted freedom and Roman citizenship. To mark the occasion, the Senator's son presented Fidelis a toga. Fidelis knew the toga could only be worn by free men, so he humbly accepted the gift. Both Titus and Livia cheered and hugged their father. Fidelis was overwhelmed when he was told he would be paid to manage the vineyards. An amount was not discussed. He felt so blessed! His first thought was that he should make a sacrifice to the gods but he didn't know which one to approach. On second thought, he told himself, "I don't have anything to use for a sacrifice so why am I worrying about which god to sacrifice to. I do thank whichever god arranged for my freedom."

It did not take long for Fidelis to realize that as a free man, he could now control his future, but his children were not as fortunate. Freedom had made him eligible to use the public baths whenever he wanted. Yet, he rarely took advantage of the baths because Titus did not have the same right. His children being slaves while he was a free man was upsetting to him. But there was little he could do to obtain freedom for his children. He did not have the money to buy their freedom. He could only try to persuade the senator's family to free them.

Every time the opportunity presented itself for Fidelis to talk about freedom for his children, the Senator's son always had other things that demanded his attention.

When Fidelis was finally successful in getting the son's attention, the son said, "Fidelis, what difference would it make? You and your family have always been well treated and all of you come and go as you want. That will continue whether they are free or not. I don't see where freeing them would change anything for them. But

I will consider it at another time when I don't have such pressing issues facing me."

Fidelis would try again some other time. He continued living in the same home with Titus and Livia, unusual as it was. Other people thought how strange that a free man would live in the same home with slaves. But to Fidelis, family was important and he was convinced that someday freedom would be granted to his children. Until then he relied upon the fondness that had developed through prior years between him and the senator's children to keep his family together. The three of them had been together since Titus was born except for the year Livia was married.

When Titus had turned 17, his sister had a marriage arranged by the Senator's son. However, her husband, who worked for Fidelis, was tragically killed soon after when a cart loaded with grapes overturned on him, crushing his chest. So, she came back to live with Titus and their father.

Fidelis continually struggled with the fact that he was a free man and his children were still slaves. One evening he and Titus had a conversation about how freedom from slavery might be obtained for Titus and Livia. Fidelis told Titus, "I don't think the Senator's children are against granting your freedom. Your status is just not important to them."

"That is all right Father. I'm here with you and I don't think they would sell me."

"That may be true, Titus, but the thought of me being free and you a slave is very upsetting to me. Besides, things change and we have no control over what could happen."

"Well, this is the way it is and we can't change it."

"Maybe we can. How would you feel about becoming a soldier?"

"What are you talking about?"

"I learned that if you became a soldier, you would be given Roman citizenship which would require that you would be freed first."

"Father if I joined the army, I would not be here to help you. I don't know how long I would be in the army, probably for years. You are too old to do the heavy work and there would be no one to help you. No, that is not a good idea."

"I realize that, but you would be a free man and a citizen. That is what I want for you."

"I don't see how that is going to happen. I would need permission to join and I doubt if that would be given since freeing me isn't happening. And what about Livia? My joining does nothing for her".

"One thing at a time. Let me handle getting you permission, and then I will do something to gain freedom for Livia. Are you willing to join the army?"

After a long pause, Titus answered, "Yes."

"Good. I think I know how this could work for you, and I'll continue asking for Livia's freedom if it does."

The next morning, Fidelis walked to the domus. An hour later he returned, all smiles. Titus would be granted freedom and permission to join the army. Titus saw his father coming and walked out to meet him. He saw the smile on his father's face. "Well?" he asked.

Fidelus blurted out the good news. "Tomorrow, you will be a free man!"

"Father, how did you get them to agree so quickly?"

"I just pointed out how providing a man for the army could put the family in a favorable position and make them look good to the upper wealthy class. Since their father's death, the family has lost some social status. This might help to get them noticed in their circle of friends. They thought about it and agreed. They said, 'The papers will be drawn up tomorrow.'"

Titus was surprised and excited at the same time. Fidelis was all smiles yet was thinking to himself, "Who will help me harvest the grapes?" The same thought was on Titus' mind. He asked, "Father if I go now, who is going to help you harvest the grapes?"

"Don't you think about harvesting grapes. There are others on this property who can help harvest grapes. Titus, from now on you will make the decisions as to where you go and what you do. No longer will someone else control your future. First, you just think about being a good army man, whatever they are called."

They walked back into their home with their arms across each other's shoulders. Livia looked at both of them and could tell something was about to happen. She just had no idea what.

Titus gently held her hands while he told her he was leaving to join the army of Rome. Livia, who knew nothing about the army, began crying when Titus finished telling her his plans. Titus never expected that reaction from his sister. His jaw dropped. Her sobs touched him deeply, and he began to have second thoughts about leaving. Suddenly, he had an emotional feeling he had never felt before. He feared the loss of family unity and love could happen. In an effort to console her, he said, "I will be fine and so will you. I'll return before you realize I'm gone."

"No, you won't and it just will not be the same without you here, Titus."

"I'm sure it will be different. You are strong and will adapt to the change without any problem. It will just take a little getting used to my absence."

The next day the sun never seemed so bright. Titus walked back and forth while he waited for the papers that granted him permission to join the army. He began to feel that he had walked his legs down to his knees. While he waited, he put what few things he owned on a blanket and rolled it up. Livia prepared some food for Titus to take. When she gave it to him, words escaped her and her eyes began to water. She just turned and walked away.

"Livia, wait!"

She just kept walking. For the second time Titus felt emotions he had never experienced before. He just stood and watched his sister walk away.

It was mid-morning when Fidelis returned and handed Titus his freedom papers. Titus looked at his father who was all smiles. He said, "Go Titus and always do your best. You are now a Roman citizen."

Titus said nothing, he just had a large lump in his throat. They clasped one another and said goodbye. He could not face his sister again, so he picked up the blanket and the food then looked around one more time before walking out the door. Titus began a journey that would change his life. The small family of three had been together for 19 years. Now he was alone and walking into a new and different life.

Suddenly his heart was heavy, thinking about his father and sister. He had never experienced life without them. He stopped. He almost turned around to walk back. But then he remembered he was now free and a citizen. He began wondering what it would be like being a soldier. What would the training be like? He began walking again.

He was glad it was springtime, when life seems to start anew, as he was about to do. The first night, he found shelter in a deserted gardening shed. He spread out the blanket he had brought and opened the food his sister had given him. This made him think of his father and sister again. He ate very little before he laid down on the blanket. He was grateful it was not winter.

II

Transition

After a two-day walk and asking for directions several times, Titus arrived at a training castrum for legionaries. It was the third morning since he left home. Shortly after sunup, not knowing what to do, he just stood on the road leading into the base and stared. Yesterday he had eaten the last of the food his sister had given him. He was hungry and totally lacking in confidence. A sentry watched him for several minutes, then approached and questioned his intentions.

Titus stammered out, "I want to join the army."

The sentry said, "Follow me." and led Titus to a building not far from the entry to the castrum and told him to go inside and report to the soldier sitting at the table. Inside, Titus repeated his desire to join the army.

The soldier at the table said, "Do you know when you sign, you will be committing to 20 years?"

Titus was surprised and froze for a minute. He had not expected this, yet he had committed to joining. He said, "No, I didn't." He paused, then said, "But I still want to join."

"Do you have papers to prove you are over 17 years of age and a free man?" Titus was asked.

"Yes, I do," he said as he handed over the papers his father had given him just before he left.

The soldier looked over the papers, then entered the name of Titus Cornelius on a scroll and told Titus to follow him. They walked into a large room containing stacks of tunics, and breastplates of leather and metal. Behind them there were racks holding swords with a girdle attached. Across the back wall were lances leaning upright. On another wall hung shields made of wood and leather. Titus had no idea that so many weapon accessories existed and in such large quantities. He stood with his mouth open. The soldier said, "Keep moving".

He was passed on to a burly unshaven fellow twice his age. This man, in his mind's eye, seemed to be sizing Titus Cornelius up. Titus was taller and more muscular than the other recruits he had processed. Then the burly man started issuing him some clothing and all the weapons of war. After basic instructions were given about caring for weapons he had been issued, he was told, "If you lose any weapon the replacement cost will be deducted from your pay of 900 sasterces, some of which you will receive four times a year. Now go and report to your instructor." He was led away by another soldier.

He awkwardly left, holding everything he had been given very tightly. What to do with the lance he had been given puzzled Titus. He didn't know whether to carry it straight up or point it forward or maybe backwards. He tried all three, and struggled to keep up with the soldier leading him.

The soldier led him outside, to an open area where there were 13 other men, all strangers, who looked as lost as he did. They stood, holding everything they had been issued, smiling at each other but saying nothing.

Titus had not been standing there long when an older soldier walked up and said to the group, "I will be your instructor while you are in training. All of you are expected to follow my instructions without question. Anyone who does not, will receive 15 lashes. Now put your gear down and line up, tirones!"

Titus had never heard that word before and wondered what tirones meant. Whatever it meant, the instructor's voice made it obvious that it applied to him. His brain was processing new words and situations. *The instructor saying to do what I say or you will get 15 lashes, must be meant to scare us. I was never whipped as a slave, and this is a higher status than slavery.*

Each man held on to his newly issued weapons and tunics, not knowing where to put them or how to keep them separated from the others. Finally, after some exasperating moments, they just dropped them on the ground. There was no other choice. The instructor, Breanus, watched with quiet amusement.

After they aligned themselves as they thought best, the instructor announced, "All of you are to swear an oath to Caesar and Rome. Repeat after me: I will serve Caesar and Rome under all conditions." The recruits repeated the words.

"By following all orders given to me by my superiors." Again, the recruits repeated the words.

"Giving my life if need be for Rome's glory." There was silence.

No one continued repeating the oath. They were all stunned at the depth of the oath. They understood what it required, and accepting it was more than they had anticipated. Cornelius, as well as the other men, felt a sinking feeling in the pit of his stomach. The realization hit all of them that they were not only giving up some of their personal freedom of choice, they were also putting their lives in the hands of someone else. That was frightening!

Each of the new tirones were weighing the impact of this statement. Titus's thoughts were on the short length of time he had experienced freedom. Now, he would be submitting to a new authority. Yet it seemed different because he had a choice in answering whereas as a slave, he had no choices. If he did not repeat the words, he would be rejected from the army and that would break the condition for his freedom. If he did repeat the words, he felt he would be submitting to the army some of his newly granted freedoms. He realized that freedom of choices had consequences.

Breanus had experienced this reaction before. He looked directly into the eyes of each man and said, "You are Roman tirones now. You will be Roman Legionaries when you complete this training. Much is demanded of you and much is expected from you. After you have completed basic training, you will find you are treated with respect from fellow soldiers and from Roman citizens. You are joining an elite group of men who have made this pledge.

"Glory will be yours for outstanding service! Punishment will be given for disobedience. If you desert, you will be caught and run through with a sword. Now, this is an order. Repeat after me: giving my life if need be for Rome's glory." Slowly one man began, then another repeated the words. Then the other 12 voices joined in and completed every word of the oath.

"Good! You will be under my direction for the next three months. I intend to make you into Legionaries. If you do what I command and apply yourself, you will be a Legionary.

"While you are here, you will sleep in the building behind you. Inside there are shelves on the walls where you are to keep anything that you will not need for the day's activities. Behind this building are some fire pits where you can prepare the food that will be given to you. The cost of that food will be deducted from your pay. Forty paces beyond the fire pits is a ditch to relieve yourselves. Any questions?"

There were none. The new recruits were intimidated by their instructor.

"Alright, pair up with someone who will be your training partner throughout your time here. Then the two of you go inside and pick your spots to sleep and deposit your gear in whatever place you have selected. Do it quickly, then come back to me. A warning! If anyone takes anything from another Tirone, their punishment will be severe. When you return you are going to learn how to march!" The group started mingling together, asking questions of each other.

Cornelius thought, "How can I train with a man I know nothing about? Maybe there is someone who has worked in a vineyard. At least I would have something in common with such a person." After asking around, he could find no one who had worked in a vineyard. However, one man by the name Primus Constant did say, "I never worked in a vineyard, but my family raised vegetables to sell. I know about the earth and gardening."

Cornelius decided there were at least some similarities in their backgrounds. So, he asked Constant to be his training partner. Constant was 15 centimeters shorter than Cornelius and had the typical Roman features of a dark skin and a prominent nose. His muscular body was evidence of being a laborer. The two men soon became more than training partners; they would become lifelong friends.

All 14 returned to face the instructor within the allotted time. When asked if everyone had chosen a partner, there were six men who had not paired with someone. Breanus said, "When I told you to pair up, that was what I meant! You six will march around the parade ground 50 times after everyone else is dismissed. By the time you have completed your special march, you better have your partner selected."

Now all of you will march over to the commissary to obtain your food rations. Form four lines facing the east. When I say march, you are to start walking, beginning with your left foot. Keep enough space between you and the man in front of you so you will not step on him. When I say halt, you are to stop."

Before they moved, Breanus reorganized them from one line to four lines of three men with two lines having one extra man. Titus was placed first in one of the lines because he was 9 centimeters taller than the other men. The command was given, "March!" The lines started well enough, but problems soon occurred because each man's stride was different. "Halt!" Some froze immediately while some took another step. A few bumped into the man in front of them.

"We will try again. Your step should be 46 centimeters. Keep the same space between you and the man in front; also keep in position with the men on your left and right. March!"

There was some improvement but not enough. Breanus stopped them again and barked some more instructions. The third time the group made it to the commissary, though without military precision.

Breanus said, "You move like three legged camels. You are going to do better if I have to march you all day and all night. Now go inside and get your rations, then form up where you stand now."

Each man was given a ration of wheat, rice, some dried meat, cheese, some vegetables, a container of wine and a small metal pot. There were bags on a table for them to use to carry their rations. Lastly, each man was to make his mark on a record to prove he had been given his rations. Titus wrote his name, which surprised Breanus and the other recruits.

Outside again, Breanus told the men, "Every day you will be given time to prepare a meal for yourself, once in the morning and once late in the day unless we are in a battle. In that case, you eat what you can when you can. Now, let's see if you can march back to the barracks without stepping on each other. Line up as you did before."

While holding their rations, they formed their lines again. Breanus said, "You just marched straight forward coming over here. Going back, we'll see if you can march around corners. So, listen, I don't want to tell you a second time. When turning a corner, the inside ranks must take shorter steps than the other three lines, until all four ranks have turned, then resume normal marching." The group started off marching straight, carrying their rations.

Two minutes later they heard, "Column left, march." The formation turned with the outside rank running to catch up because the inside rank did not take smaller steps. "Halt! You idiots! What did I just tell you? The inside rank takes half steps and the second rank takes shorter steps until the other two ranks have turned. Keep even with the man on your left and the man on your right. Try it again." They did better the next time. And even better yet the third time. They all felt good about their progress until they heard, "Column right, march." The outside rank had to run to keep up. "Halt! Are you all stupid? I'll repeat the instructions one more time. Anyone who makes a mistake again will march 50 times around the parade grounds."

Each man's confidence began to waver. The next right turn was made raggedly but without a mistake. It took two hours for the group to make it back to their barracks without being stopped for correction. Finally, they made it. Relief could be seen in their faces.

Breanus barked, "Take your rations inside and return to the lineup. There is still daylight and you have a lot to learn."

Back in line they heard Breanus describe legionaries in glowing terms. "Legionaries are elite soldiers. They are better trained and are more fit than any other known army. They can march seven schoenus a day, prepare a camp with a defensive battlement, then get up the next day and do it all over again."

The rest of the day was spent learning about work details, guard duty, and road patrols; all of which they would be assigned to perform from time to time. They were told the bathhouse would be available for them to use when they were off duty if it was not in use by the officers.

As the sun approached the horizon, Cornelius and Constant were looking at one another and thinking, "Would instructions and rules never end?" Finally, the day did end with the instructor saying, "Every day begins with a muster parade. You are to be fully dressed, with your weapons and in position before the 2nd hour begins. We will march with all the other units on the base in a parade formation. I expect you to march as precisely as the other contubernias. If you embarrass me with marching mistakes, you will be extremely sorry." With that they were dismissed for the day. They scattered in different directions as if escaping from some powerful foe.

Primus Constant and Titus Cornelius remained in place. They saw nothing to run away from. Then they realized they were alone, so they followed the other men to the pits. Primus said to Titus, "I can't say I am hungry right now, are you?" Most of the other men were gathering around the fire pits and starting to prepare their meals.

Cornelius said, "No, I was earlier, but with all that happened today, I forgot about food. Now, I'm not. Besides I don't think there is any room for us at the fire pits. Why don't we wait until the others are finished, then we will have plenty of room to eat. This will give us a chance to talk so we can get to know each other a little better. Tell me, do you know anything about army life? I don't."

"All I know about the army is watching a parade of soldiers marching by after some battle some place. I never gave any thought about learning how to march, or about what their daily living requirements might be."

"It is the same with me. That is all I can remember, seeing a parade with the army marching by and a lot of cheering people. I always wondered if the people were cheering because they had won a battle or because of the precision of the marchers."

"Did you notice there was always one man in front of each group of men? He was always dressed differently and had a helmet with strands of hair or feathers on it. He must be their leader."

"I'm not sure, but I think he is called a centurion. I'm sure we will find out before long."

"Cornelius, what do you think tomorrow will be like?"

"I guess we will do more marching. We were not very good today. Maybe we will start learning how to use a sword. I'm looking forward to that."

"Really. I know we will learn how to use a sword, but the thought of killing another man is upsetting to me."

"I don't disagree with you Constant, but someday we will be in a situation where it is kill, or be killed and I don't want to be the one killed."

Constant frowned, "I guess you are right. I just had not considered fighting to the death until now."

"Think of it this way, if you do not kill him, he is going to kill you. It is a matter of survival."

"That is good, I'll remember that." Changing the conversation, Constant asked, "Where are you from, Cornelius?"

"Near a town called Volterra. Where is your home?"

"I lived in Potenza. My family has been there for the last three generations. My father and his father raise vegetables on their farm near there. That is where I grew up. My father taught me about planting and raising vegetables. When you asked if anyone had worked in a vineyard, I thought there might be some similarities between vineyard work and raising vegetables. Tell me does your family own a vineyard?"

"Well, they don't own a vineyard but my father has been in control of one owned by a senator for several years. I hope to own one someday."

"Wow! Your father worked for a senator? Did you ever get to meet him?"

"Yes, I would see him from time to time. But seeing a senator doesn't mean anything."

"I have never been near anyone of importance like you have. And I saw you can write your name. You are not like the rest of us, Cornelius."

"Yes I am. I'm just a common worker like everyone else here."

Constant said, "You amaze me. How did you learn to write?"

"I only know how to write because my father was a teacher. He taught me to write and read."

"You read as well as write? I don't think you will remain a foot soldier."

"I doubt it will make any difference, but I hope to do other things. As for writing your name, that is not difficult. I can teach you if you want to learn."

"Thanks for the offer but not now. Learning to be a soldier is enough for me. Cornelius, why did you join the army? Being able to read and write, I would think you could do lots of other things."

Titus was silent for a moment, then he said, "What you don't know is, I joined the army so I could obtain freedom and Roman citizenship. That is the only reason I joined."

"What are you saying?"

"I told you my father was a teacher; but I didn't tell you that he was a slave as well, and so was I. He had been granted freedom and citizenship and he wanted me to have the same thing. So did I. My owner agreed to free me if I joined the army. That is why I am here. Does knowing this change your opinion of me?"

Constant was a little surprised; he answered, "No, it doesn't. What you were is not as important as what you are now and maybe what you are going to be. I have always been free, but I don't know how to write. You were a slave who could write and now you are a free man. This is unbelievable."

"You are a wise man, Constant."

As darkness closed in, Cornelius and Constant prepared their meal and continued their conversation while eating. Cornelius said,

"If we are going to be side by side for three months or more, let's call one another by our first name. My name is Titus. What is your first name?"

"Mine is Primus, and thank you. I feel better." They smiled at each other and washed out their pots. Day one of life in the Roman army was over.

The following day, Titus and Primus were dressed with weapons in hand before the 2nd hour began. They lined up as they had the day before. Titus looked around and noticed the other groups lining up had only eight to ten men. They were made up of older looking men whose clothing and shields were worn. It was obvious that the men in the other groups had been in service for some time. To them, this parade was just another routine task.

After all groups had formed up, a chariot pulled by two horses sped by Titus' group. There was a man in the chariot who was dressed in finer clothing than the soldiers in formation. When he stopped in front of all the men, he turned and raised one arm. Then he dropped it, a trumpet sounded, and one word echoed back through the ranks; "March!"

All the formations started marching around a large open area, called the parade ground. The recruits were the last group in the parade line up. When they passed by a large raised platform, the man in the chariot raised his sword and yelled, "Hail Caesar!" After marching around the field a second time, all groups were dismissed except the recruits. They marched back to their quarters, stored their weapons, and reported to their instructor.

Breanus marched them for an hour. Then he had them run for half an hour. No more had they stopped when they were told to march for another hour. Running again for half an hour was ordered without any break. This cycle was repeated three times. Some were not only breathing hard; they were having trouble keeping up.

Breathlessly Primus whispered to Titus, "Why is that soldier with a long pole following us?"

Titus answered, "I don't know."

"Quiet!" the man with the pole yelled out. After marching and running for 3 hours, they learned with regret the purpose of the man with a pole. If anyone slowed down and begin to fall behind, the man with the pole began beating the straggler and continued to do so until the tirone returned to his place in line.

When Breanus felt the group had made enough progress in marching, he stopped the exercise. Without any break the men were told to jump as high as they could. Then they were told to jump as far as they could. These instructions were repeated for the next hour. The instructor kept saying, "Someday you will have to jump over a wall or cross a ditch while fighting an enemy. If you fall, you will be dead."

Next the tirones were given wooden swords and shields and instructed on how to hold and swing a sword. Then each man faced a post five feet tall. This would be his adversary. Against the post each tirone learned how to strike his sword, extend it forward, and lunge with it. Lastly, instructions were given on defensive maneuvers.

For seven days, marching and exercising was their daily routine until Breanus was satisfied. Then they were commanded to pair with their partner. They were pitted against one another in mock battles. The men learned how to defend themselves and how to attack another, but not before most had bruises and sore hands

Then came a day of welcome relief. The requirement that day was swimming. Those who could not swim were given instructions. Those who already knew how to swim were allowed to swim or watch. For most it was a day of enjoyment. Just a few struggled before completing the swimming requirement.

Additional assignments of guard duty or a work detail did not relieve one from the daily training exercises. On those days a recruit would be so tired at the end of the day, that he would literally collapse on his bed.

One day was set aside to learn military organization and rank. Breanus began, "When you finish your basic training, each of you will be placed in a contubernium of eight to ten men which will be led by a decanus. There are 10 contubernias in a centuria, which will be led by a centurion and an optio. This is the main fighting group. Six centurions form a cohort. The senior centurion leads the cohort. The highest level is a legion, which contains nine cohorts. A legion is led by legate and a tribune. Whenever you are in the presence of an optio, a centurion or a tribune, you will salute them by placing your right arm across your chest."

The next day they returned to the daily routine of marching, exercising, and mock battles. At day's end, they learned of a new requirement. Breanus said, "In the morning there will be a 6-hour march. Bring all your weapons, all your food rations, and extra clothes. You must carry them on this march. This march must be completed within the six hours. At the end of the march, you will prepare defenses for a camp. The return march does not have to be completed in six hours."

Even though the morning began with rain, the march still began at the break of dawn. Before the end of the six hours, they arrived at their targeted location expecting a rest. Almost immediately, the order was given, "Prepare the defenses." Shovels appeared and dirt began to pile up around the camp. When the mound was all the way around the camp, they were permitted to rest. After a short rest and some food, they were told to form up for the march back. The return trip back to the main costrum went slower and it was well after dark when the men arrived at their barracks. The tirones were tired but relieved because they had survived the march. Another milestone completed.

Their last phase of training was learning battle formations for small groups, a centuria, and for cohorts. One of the main formations was the testudo. In this formation, the men held their shields over their heads to form an interlocking 'roof', while the soldiers in front held their shields in front of them to form a wall. Lances protruded outward from the first line. The formation would advance at a steady pace. This and other formations were practiced over and over.

After three months were over, the tirones were told, "You are now ready to become part of the world's greatest military fighting force. You have been trained to be superior to any other army. Go and honor Caesar and Rome." Every man felt proud of his accomplishment.

They were assigned into different contubernias as replacements. Titus and Primus were placed in separate groups but in the same centuria.

As they gathered together their belongings and weapons and left the barracks, Titus and Primus clasped arms and vowed to remain in contact with each other as much as possible. They moved to separate barracks and met the men they would be serving with.

Two years would pass in a period of peace. Titus found himself repairing roads daily, and moving around to wherever there was a need. A change finally occurred when he was told that he was assigned to a group building a new bridge. He was glad because he would be in the same place for a while. Days would be more routine.

Whenever free time allowed, which was rare, Titus and Primus would get together, usually for drinking and the telling of crude jokes. If time would allow, they searched for women to spend the night with.

III

The War Years

In the year 14 AD, Emperor Augustus Caesar died. Members of the royal family began a power struggle for the right to rule the empire. At the same time the army was in a rebellious mood because some legions had not been paid for several months. These legions were on the brink of revolting. Other legions began aligning themselves with one family member or another. The empire's army was distracted from protecting the nation.

It was during this time the empire suffered the defeat of three legions in Germania. Thousands of Roman soldiers were killed or captured. This was a terrible disaster for the world's greatest army. Rome's pride was crushed. Many of the army officers had revenge on their minds for several years. In this unstable environment Tiberius, the stepson of Augustus, surfaced as the strongest of the squabbling families of power. He became the new Caesar. The political situation was resolved but the precarious situation in the army remained.

A year later, Titus Cornelius' legion was stationed just outside of Rome. He had been with this legion for 2 years. This legion had remained loyal to Tiberius during the power struggles. Their legate was Germanicus.

While all these struggles were taking place, Titus Cornelius and Primus Constant had no interest in the royal power struggle or any of the army's problems. Their concerns were with day-to-day issues in their lives. They met together occasionally, sometimes drinking too much but never causing problems for themselves. They shared news and rumors. Eventually, their conversations always got around to the defeat of the northern army. Of lesser importance were the rumors of the political instability. They did not know who was going to become the new Caesar and really did not care. It would make little difference to them. Nor did they have any interest in the legions about to revolt because of lack of pay. They had been paid regularly. They were only concerned with what was involved in their daily lives.

During one occasion, Primus asked Titus, "Do you think we will ever avenge the army's loss to the barbarians?"

"I know that was some years ago, but sooner or later we will march against them. I just have no idea when. All of my superiors talk about it. It is obvious they feel that the loss was unacceptable and must be avenged."

Primus said, "Well, if we do, do you think all legions will march north against the barbarians?"

"I have no way of knowing. I'm not in charge. Why do you ask?"

" I'm not sure they will, because I heard that some soldiers have not been paid, so they are not following orders."

"Where did you hear that?" Titus asked.

"I overheard two of our decani talking about problems in the northern legions."

Titus said, "That is hard to believe. Every man took an oath to be loyal. We have always been paid. Sometimes it was slow but we were paid. Maybe I don't understand why there is a problem. As for what legions might go north, my guess is not all legions would go but enough will go to assure victory."

Primus asked, "Do you think we will go?"

"Primus, I don't know. We'll find out in due time. You sound as if you want to go fight."

"I do! I have never been in a real battle. I want to experience that."

Unknown to the two of them, Germanicus, who was held in high regard by Tiberius, was meeting with him at that very moment. They were discussing what to do about the legions on the verge of revolting. Germanicus was honored by being made Legatus Legionis. Then he was ordered to subdue the insubordinate legions in any way he saw fit. After the meeting he quickly returned to his headquarters and summoned all his officers.

He told them, "There are three legions that are about to revolt. It is up to us to prevent this. I hope to do so without any bloodshed. However, if it comes to that, your troops must be willing to fight against their fellow countrymen. No one wants to fight against his own countryman, but these rebels want to tear down what the army stands for. We should not think of them as fellow countrymen as long as that is their attitude. Our army must be unified and any rebellious thinking suppressed. Return to your men and prepare them to face the possibility of killing a fellow Roman. Make sure they understand. Then prepare them ready to march against these rebellious legions. If any soldier is not up to killing his countryman if necessary, then you are to kill that man. Any weakness in following orders will not be tolerated. Tomorrow we march at sunrise."

When Titus heard the news, he was shocked. He asked himself, "Can I fight and kill someone I might have known in basic training or any other countryman? I hope it does not come to that." He wanted to talk to Primus, but time did not allow it. At sunrise, five legions marched north.

In the rebellious legions, discipline was very lax and there were very few guards posted. Germanicus's five legions surrounded them before they realized what was happening. Germanicus called for a meeting with the rebellious officers. He heard their complaints.

Some of the complaints he thought were reasonable, but others he dismissed.

He told them, "I will address those grievances I feel are valid. I will also guarantee you will be paid even if I have to do it out of my own funds. In exchange, you will honor our code of discipline and loyalty to Rome. If you do not do so, my legions will completely destroy your legions. The decision is yours."

Knowing they were surrounded and outnumbered, the rebellious officers huddled together and quietly talked. It did not take long for them to decide. "We understand and thank you for hearing us out. We choose loyalty to Rome." With that, they renewed their vows to Rome and Caesar.

The officers returned to their men and explained the situation, including the alternatives. Very few were willing to fight a superior force. The officers had every man in their commands renew the same vow. There was still some grumbling and uneasiness, but no major problem erupted.

Both groups made camp next to one another that night and a lull settled over both sides. But suspicions slowly started to grow. After their side of the confrontation had settled into a camp, Titus and Primus were able to meet for the first time since they had marched north. Their first conversation discussed the possibility of killing a fellow countryman.

"Titus, do you think you could have killed a fellow soldier?"

Titus answered Primus, "I will never know. If one was attacking me, I think I could. But if I was ordered to kill one, I don't know. I am just glad it did not come to that. But now I'm not sure if I trust those men in the rebellious legions or not."

"I agree with you. I don't think I could trust them either." said Primus.

Germanicus knew there was grumbling and pent-up emotions among the soldiers on both sides. Something was needed to release those emotions and to bind the army together. He ordered all the soldiers into legion formation, mounted his horse, and began to address them as he rode back and forth in front of the formations. "I know not all of you can hear what I say, so I ask those who can hear to share what I say to those who cannot hear."

Then he continued, "We are now brothers in arms and reunited into a Roman army. What has taken place needs to be forgotten! For now, we march against our common enemy, the Germanic barbarians. We have endured defeat at the Battle of the Teutobury Forest long enough. What we do now begins our revenge of that loss. After we are victorious, you may take any of the enemy's property you want. This includes the women as well. At sunrise we march against the Marsi tribe. Hail Caesar!"

There was a loud cheer! "Hail Caesar!"

Titus was excited. He knew Primus would be too. This would be their first encounter with an enemy. He sharpened his sword, tested his lance, and cleaned his shield. Anticipation and excitement charged him up so much that sleep eluded him.

At sunrise the soldiers lined up in marching formation and marched the entire day. When they stopped that evening to prepare their evening meal, all the centurions addressed their troops. "At first light in the morning, be ready to attack the villages of the Marsi. We will completely destroy them. There are to be no prisoners taken."

When morning came, the soldiers formed into the centurial battle formation of three rows and charged the village. Opposition was light, and the village was quickly taken and totally destroyed. The Romans suffered no losses while no barbarian lives were spared. On they went into the next village. This time the German barbarians were not surprised and were better prepared for the attackers.

The fighting began with the first row of legionaries charging the enemy. Many were killed on both sides. The second row attacked very shortly after the first row. It was followed by a third row.

Titus was in the first row and one of the first to engage the enemy. He promptly killed one, then two. Adrenaline roared through his body. He ran forward swinging his sword, slashing and cutting whoever was in front of him. His lance was stuck in an enemy somewhere behind him. At the end of the day, he was splattered with his enemies' blood and very little of his own. His aggressive efforts had been noticed by his fellow legionaries. He became an example of aggressiveness and strength to the other soldiers.

After two more days of fighting, four villages were conquered. The advance stopped because the winter winds were beginning to blow. The army began a withdrawal to what would be their winter quarters. Along the way they successfully fought through another opposing tribe. As the fighting subsided, the soldiers started accumulating the spoils of war. Several young attractive women were also forced to accompany them.

The legionaries' spirits were very high. Titus was tired but felt exhilarated. He spent little time searching for any spoils. He picked up few things as he walked along the way. While he walked, it became clear to him that the army was his calling.

The Roman army's efforts at killing and destroying the German barbarians were so complete that their attacks could be classified as massacres. However, from the Roman viewpoint, not only had Germanicus accomplished his purposes of re-establishing rebelling legions, he had begun avenging the army's earlier defeat at the Battle of the Teutobury Forest. The Roman defeat of the Germans had weakened the Germanic tribes to the point they could not be a major challenge to the Roman Empire any longer. Yet there were still numerous German warriors scattered across the land that must be dealt with.

Also, the uneasiness among the soldiers was completely gone. They were so tired that there was no thought of fighting each other. The victory, along with the spoils gained, had restored the discontented legionaries' loyalty to Rome and to Germanicus personally.

Titus Cornelius's performance had been so outstanding, his decanus verbally praised him in front of the other soldiers, "The way you saw Titus Cornelius fight is what I expect from all of you." Titus was embarrassed.

When they reached the area where their winter camp would be, he also praised Cornelius to their centurion, stating how Titus Cornelius had been an outstanding fighter. The decanus said, "With men like Cornelius, my contubernia can handle any enemy."

Life in the field during winter months was difficult for the army. The sun refused to appear in the sky for weeks at a time. Snows came, and many times there was a strong wind, resulting in mountains of drifted snow. This made any troop movement almost impossible. Each day seemed to grow colder and more difficult for daily life.

The men spent most of their time cutting down trees for firewood to keep them warm. Both days and nights were spent with men wrapped in robes or any kind of coverage that would keep them warm. Trying to keep warm and healthy was not easy but the brutal winter provided a rest from fighting and time for wounds to heal.

Titus and Primus, wearing everything they had, met a few times. They always asked if the other was well and if he had food. They exchanged stories of their recent encounter with the Germans. They both had come through the battles with only superficial injuries, for which they were grateful. They praised their gods for giving them protection. Both had acquired valuable items as spoils. Primus had even taken a woman but Titus had not.

"Why didn't you take a woman, Titus? She could cook and definitely would keep you warm at night."

"I don't want a woman. I am so pumped up from the battles that I don't want to be distracted by a woman."

"You're a strange one, Titus. Only you and a few officers don't have a woman."

Titus replied, "Right now, there are other things that are more important than a woman, that's all."

After three months the snow changed to rain. Each day got a little warmer than the day before and the rains came less frequent. Attitudes began to improve, and the men became restless. With the coming of spring, a new campaign against the Germans was planned.

What to do with the captive women was only a minor problem to these soldiers. They could not be left behind, for they would take or destroy everything left in the winter camp. Most of the soldiers' personal items and the spoils they had obtained would be left in camp until the campaign was over. Therefore, most of the women were told to go and not come back. They would be killed if they returned.

Some were killed. Yet in a few rare cases love had developed between soldier and woman. In these cases, the woman became an unauthorized "wife". These few were allowed to stay behind and each one hoped her man would return. A few men were left as guards for the winter camp.

Before Germanicus led the men across the Rhine River, he fired them up by repeating what had happened at the Battle of Teutoburg Forest. He reminded them of their good work during the last battles; and, now the enemy's defeat would be complete and Rome's past loss would be fully avenged.

After crossing the river, they pillaged the countryside and attacked the Chatti tribe. By nightfall the Legionaries had broken through the outer defenses of their capital, Mattium. The following morning began with the capture of the wife of Arminius, the most prominent German. Then they went through the city pillaging and killing. At the end of the day, all the citizens of the capital were dead. After two days of fighting, the army withdrew to rest and address their wounds.

Once again Titus Cornelius gained more notoriety for his fighting skills and the legions marched back to their camp victorious. Tiberius was so pleased learn of Germanicus's victories, that he added another adjective, Imperator, to Germanicus' rank.

The German barbarian leader, Arminius, was furious and united all the remaining Germanic tribes to face the Romans. The two forces met on the plains of Idistaviso near the Weser River. The battle raged on all day. By mid-day, both sides began breaking apart. Fighting became pockets of an individual against an individual. Titus's contubernium found themselves separated from their centuria and surrounded by the Germans. Four legionaries were killed in the first charge by the Germans and three were seriously wounded.

Titus almost single handedly held off the Germans. He was fighting two Germans when help arrived. The remaining barbarians fled from the arriving Legionaries. The rescuers saw Titus was standing over the top of his wounded decanus in a protective stance, blood dripping from his sword, his body covered with a mixture of his blood and that of his enemies. There was a gash in his left leg and a large cut on his right arm. Blood trickled down the left side of his head from an open wound. Titus stepped forward and fell to his knees as help arrived. He was exhausted.

After checking the bodies, only Titus, his decanus, and one other legionary remained alive. All around the three were dead Germans. Two survivors had to be carried back to their camp. Titus limped back with assistance.

That night after a short rest, Titus treated his wounds as best he could. His body ached but he told his newly assigned decanus he would be ready by morning. The decanus said, "Titus you have earned the right to be excused from tomorrow's battle". Titus made no comment but when morning came, he was in his place in the formation. Admiration for him was in every legionary's mind.

In battle after battle Titus' bravery and fighting skills were noticed and his notoriety spread. As a reward, Titus Cornelius was made a decanus. Even Germanicus heard of Titus Cornelius's feats. He was impressed and sent word for Cornelius to come to his tent. Titus asked the messenger why Germanicus wanted to see him? He was worried he had done something wrong and was about to be punished. The messenger said he did not know.

He was nervous as he entered Germanicus' tent. He gave the proper salute. His mouth was so dry he could not speak. Germanicus smiled and sensing Cornelius' uneasiness he said, "You are not in any trouble. You are here because of what I have heard about you. Is what I have heard about your fighting skills all true?"

Although Titus Cornelius felt relief, he was still nervous and had trouble answering. His mouth was moving, but nothing was coming out. Germanicus again smiled and told his servant to give Cornelius some wine. After drinking it, Titus Cornelius was able to answer, "I don't know what you have heard, sir. I can only say I have always fought to the best of my abilities."

"Seems that you are not only a good soldier, you are humble as well. Tell me, how long have you been in the army?"

"I am in my seventh year, sir."

Germanicus replied, "You have done well. After seeing you, I can only believe what I have heard is true. I just wanted to see what you looked like. You should have a good future in the army. Stay alive young man. Rome needs good legionaries like you. You may go now." Titus saluted and walked out. He exhaled and thought, "I can't believe I saw Germanicus so close and alone. Primus will never believe this." However, telling Primus would have to wait.

There were still many small German groups roaming the countryside. Germanicus planned a new campaign against the remaining

Germans. The first battle lasted all day, with neither side achieving a decisive victory. Both sides were exhausted. The Germans drew back while the Romans withdrew across the Rhine. Occasional fighting went on for two years. During this time, Titus Cornelius' reputation as a fighter continued to grow with each battle. Soldiers in other contubernias felt safer fighting beside him, and they started looking to him for leadership.

Finally, total victory against the German barbarians took place near the Angrivarian Wall. Germanicus ordered his troops to take no prisoners, for the extermination of the Germanic tribes was the only solution he saw for ending the war. After two days of fighting the final battle, the Romans were victorious. They raised a monument with the inscription: "The army of Tiberius Caesar, after thoroughly conquering all the tribes between the Rhine and the Elbe, has dedicated this monument to Mars, Jupiter, and Tiberius Caesar."

Two legions remained at the border while the others marched back toward Rome. Both Titus and Primus were in the returning group. The march was stopped just outside of Rome, and the decani were called together. They were instructed to tell their men to clean up and be prepared to march through the city the next day. The men spent the night shining shields and cleaning their togas and breastplates. When morning arrived, they lined up and marched into the city led by Germanicus in his chariot.

The streets were lined with citizens cheering and waving. As they marched along, Titus felt a surge of pride. When the parade ended and the men were dismissed, Primus started looking for Titus. When he found him, he said, "Weren't we something?"

Titus answered, "It did make me feel good. I remember being told in basic training that the people would respect us. Now I surely know it."

Primus said, "It was just as I remember seeing a victory march when I was a boy. Only this time I was not on the side watching, I was in it."

Later, after all soldiers were back in their main camp, Germanicus called for Titus Cornelius to appear before him again. This time Titus was not nervous although he did feel uncomfortable. He wore his cleanest toga and did his best to look presentable. He entered Germanicus' tent, saluted, and did a slight bow. Germanicus invited Cornelius to sit and began asking him about his family and some personal questions.

"Are you married?"

Titus answered, "No, sir. May I ask why you asked me about marriage?"

Germanicus explained, "You probably already know the army does not encourage marriage; yet there are some married men. The official policy is that miles and legionaries cannot have wives but can have a woman for needs. Officers can marry if they obtain permission to do so. If you had admitted to being married, it would have disqualified you from what I have in mind."

Titus wanted to ask what he had in mind, but Germanicus asked another question first, "Are your parents still living?"

"My father is still living, but my mother is dead." Titus wondered what all this was leading to.

"How old are you Cornelius?"

"I am 28, sir."

"A pity; I was in hopes you were 30. But no matter,"

"Why did you say that, sir?" Titus was wondering where this conversation was going.

Germanicus said, "Because, Cornelius, I think you are capable of being a centurion, and one of the requirements is being 30 years of age." Titus Cornelius' mouth dropped open. He about fell off of the stool he was sitting on. He was unable to talk or think.

Germanicus continued, "You have proven your bravery and demonstrated skill with sword and spear. You have the size and build for a centurion. If necessary, many will testify as to your valor. If I can get you an appointment, your age will not matter. But you will have to learn to read and write before I can submit your name for consideration."

Cornelius began to stammer, "Sir, I can already read and write, but I am not qualified to be a centurion."

"Good, that satisfies that requirement. As for your being qualified, no you are not, right now. However, we can teach you all you need to know. There is a training program for centurions." Germanicus called for the legion's actarius and dictated a letter to the Senate requesting that Titus Cornelius be entered into training to be a centurion. After the letter was finished, Germanicus said to Titus, "If you are approved, I will know I'm in good standing with the Senate, and you will be sent to a training program for centurions."

Cornelius just sat with his mouth open, listening but not quite believing this was actually happening. Everything swirled through his brain. "Me, a centurion? I feel confused. When I joined the army, it was a way to get freedom and I was only staying as long as necessary. That changed after this first couple of days fighting. I thought I was meant to be a soldier. But the more the fighting went on, the more I began to question this idea. I reverted back to my feeling of not staying in the army any longer than necessary. Now I could be a centurion! I think the army is going to be my life."

Germanicus said, "You may go now." Titus didn't move. Germanicus just grinned and said, "I said that is all, you may go."

Titus stood up, saluted and left Germanicus' tent somewhat puffed up. "I must tell Primus. He is not going to believe this."

He went looking for his friend. He found him just leaving the bathhouse. "Primus, you won't believe my news. I can hardly believe it myself." As they walked through the castrum, Primus could tell Titus was excited about something.

"What news? Did a relative die and leave you a fortune?"

"No, I have been selected to become a centurion!"

Primus was so surprised he stopped. Titus stood with the biggest smile he had ever had on his face.

Primus just looked at Titus. "Did I hear you right – you a centurion?"

"Yes, it's true! I can't believe it myself."

"How? I know you are a decanus, but that is a long way from a centurion. I thought it took 16 to 20 years for a soldier to go from tirone to centurion and very few have made that jump."

Titus explained, "It does, but Germanicus is asking the Senate to appoint me."

Primus questioned Titus, "Germanicus, the Legatus Legions?"

"Yes."

"You saw Germanicus, and he talked to you?" Primus was in disbelief.

Titus answered, "Yes, he called for me to go to his tent."

There was silence until Primus said, "I am glad for you, Titus. In time you will forget me but I will remember you and the good times we had together for years to come."

"I will miss the time with you as well, and I will never forget you."

Primus said, "Let's drink some wine to celebrate your good fortune. I think you should buy."

"I will buy all you can drink."

Most of the night was spent drinking, singing, and remembering highlights of past feats. Just before the sun came up on a new day, the two friends clasped arms and said goodbye. Titus watched Primus go. He suddenly felt alone. First, his father and sister were gone from his daily life, and now a great friend was walking away.

The next week Titus was informed the Senate had approved Germanicus' request. He was to leave immediately for training to be a centurion.

IV

Becoming a Centurion

As Titus made his way to the training castrum, he thought about all that had transpired since he had joined the army. He decided he had found favor with the gods, but which god? "I doubt if it was Jupiter. He is too busy to be concerned with me. It has to be Mars. I have always tried to honor all the gods, but thinking back over the last few years, I think it was Mars that protected me. What other god would have kept me from being killed? I will sacrifice to Mars once a week from now on."

He arrived at the castrum full of anxiety and excitement. After he reported to the camp commander, he was directed to the armicustos to be fitted for his armor, issued his weapons, and a cudgel, which was the sign of a centurion. A chest plate and shoulder guards would be made to his measurements. He chose the helmet he wanted, a traditional one with horsehair for a plume. He was issued a new sword with a shield and a new spear. He would have to get used to the sword being on his left side rather than his right where foot soldiers wore their swords. He was informed of a clothier on base where he could purchase cloaks and togas or any clothing he needed.

Titus expected things would be different but was surprised to learn that he would have private sleeping quarters. Never in his life had he had a bedroom to himself. Then he was amazed to hear his pay would be five times what he earned as a legionary. Before the day ended, he learned that someone would prepare his meals. He thought to himself, "What wonderful fortune has befallen me. I feel like a king!"

The next morning, he met the other candidates, who were preparing to be centurions. Some had almost completed their schooling. Others were in different stages of the training. He was the only one just beginning. He had supposed that all the others were from military backgrounds, but that was not the case. A few had come from wealthy families. They had bought their way into the program or had political connections that arranged for their appointment. These candidates were there for the prestige and notoriety. They usually quit before they finished the training program by buying their way out of the military. Cornelius had a hard time trying to be civil to these men, and he was glad to see them go.

During his time in the training camp, he stayed mostly to himself. He was friendly enough with everyone, but he made no lasting friendships. He struggled with the thought, "Do I really belong here? I wonder what these people might think if they knew I was born a slave. I have only told one man and I will tell no one else."

His training began with an interview by one of the instructors. He was treated with more respect than the basic training instructor had given him. This instructor started by asking, "Where have you served before and have you been in any battles?"

Titus' told the instructor of his experiences in the Germanic wars. The instructor was so impressed with Titus' answers he moved on to find out about Titus' abilities and battle knowledge. He found Titus fully qualified in fighting skills. The next question was, "Do you have any experiences with horses?"

Titus answered, "I have never ridden a horse, nor have I even been close to horses."

"You will be taught how to handle and ride horses." Then he asked, "Have you had any leadership experience?"

He answered, "I was a decanus for more than a year."

"That is not much experience but you will be given instructions on leadership." Further questions sought his knowledge of social etiquette and the responsibilities of a centurion. Titus had very little experience in these areas. It was obvious training would be required for these skills.

When the interview was finished, the instructor said, "You will receive instructions in four areas: leadership, horsemanship, social etiquette, and responsibilities. You must master each one or you will be disqualified. Also, your fighting skills must be verified. How long it takes to complete the course will depend on how you progress. Do you have any questions?"

"No sir, I am ready to begin."

And so, Titus began his training. He didn't realize all that was involved. First was leadership training, which also included learning about administrative duties. He just thought leadership was just leading men into battles. He quickly realized how wrong he had been.

His past leadership experience was limited to leading eight men into battle. Now, he realized there was a higher level. Not only would he be expected to lead many men into battle, he would be responsible for a victory. He would be expected to influence his subordinates to reach their highest potential.

For two weeks he learned about administration, leadership, reporting, discipline, and how to give orders. He began by reading about his new responsibilities and discussing with a tutor how responsibilities went both upward and downward. Downward was training men in his command, and upward was keeping his superiors informed of the condition of his men.

It was difficult for him to stay focused on these subjects because he was anxious to learn about battle formations and strategies. He imagined leading men into battle by different formations. However, his attention was re-focused by the end of his responsibilities training. The next assignment was to lead road patrols for two weeks. This assignment was not what he expected.

Titus was disappointed. It did not occur to him until the two weeks ended, that this was an opportunity for him to practice leadership.

One evening as he was returning from a road patrol, he was told to report to the weapons trainer in the morning. The next day the weapons trainer said, "I understand you were in the German campaign. That is good but I still need to test your skills. I want you to wrap your sword in animal skins as I have mine. This is to prevent injury to one another."

Titus did as he was told. The trainer asked, "Are you ready? If so, I want you to attack me like you would an enemy."

Titus charged the trainer with such fury that the trainer was overwhelmed. In no time, the trainer found himself on the ground with a sword at his throat. Quickly he yelled, "Enough! I will report your fighting skills have been verified."

The next session would be the most difficult for Titus. It focused on horsemanship, something entirely new to Titus. He had never had any kind of an animal in his life. After reporting to the horse instructor for the first time, he was paired with a big black mare. He stood in front of the horse, looking her in the eye and mumbling, "You are bigger than me, but I intend to be the one in control."

He began a step-by-step process, starting with how to harness a horse, then how to lead a horse. Finally, how to drive a chariot pulled by two horses. He was now beginning to feel like a centurion. Each day he gained a greater appreciation for horses. He became more at ease with them and his confidence grew. It had been a challenge for him because of his inexperience with horses.

The challenges were not over yet. A new one emerged when he was told he must not only learn to ride a horse; he must be capable of fighting from horseback. This new form of fighting slowed him down. In time he learned how to control the horse while holding a sword in one hand and a shield in the other. Only after he proved he was capable of fighting from horseback was he allowed to move on in his training.

Titus listened, applied himself, and mastered the horsemanship part of his training. As a reward, he was assigned the responsibility of leading the legionaries in the morning parade around the drill field. He remembered the first time he had witnessed a centurion doing this and how impressed he was with that centurion. He was determined to look the same. Each morning for eight days, he fully dressed and strapped on his sword. Then he mounted a chariot and drove to the front of the waiting soldiers. It was difficult for him to maintain his humility, for he no longer thought, "Do I belong here?"

Social etiquette proved to be a different challenge for Titus Cornelius. Coming from the lower class, he had little exposure to the upper class and their social rules. What little he did know came from the days of his youth. Growing up he had never lived in the Senator's house or eaten a meal with the family, but he had helped serve at meal times and on special occasions. He had seen how they treated one another and their basic manners. He remembered how guests were received and entertained. He definitely needed coaching and practice in this phase of his training.

Centurions were highly respected by civilians and held to high moral and ethical standards. Yet they could be brutal in battle or when dealing out punishment. There were civil social rules and other rules for the military culture. He had to master all of them. The areas that were covered included how to eat, how to dress, how to greet people, both civil and military, and what to do and not do in ceremonies. His test in social etiquette would occur when the Legate held his annual banquet.

He learned that once a year the Legate gave a banquet for all centurions on the castrum. Attendance was mandatory. They were to wear their best clothing and they were to bring a female. Titus was dumbfounded. He didn't know any women other than his mother and sister. Sure, he had spent some nights with other women, but they would not be acceptable for the commander's banquet. He did not know what he would do when the time came for him to attend this banquet.

Finally came the study of battle formations, strategies, attacking, and counter attacking. He learned about the attack advantage of the wedge formation and when it should be used. This formation was a triangular shape that could fan out into a wider V shape formation. There was the testudo, which was a formation where the men held their shields over their heads to form a roof, while the men in front held their shields in front of them to form a wall. He remembered this formation from his days in basic training. Back then, he had always been on the receiving end of battle orders. Now, he would be giving them. He would be totally responsible for victory or defeat. He would also be responsible for men's deaths. He had not considered that being in command could mean giving an order that would knowingly cause men to die. It was a sobering realization that weighed heavily on his mind.

During all his training days when he was not in an actual training session, he exercised and worked out with a sword or a spear. At the end of each day, he was tired and only wanted to relax at the bath house before retiring for the night, or simply just sleep. He was working harder than when he was in basic training. As a result, his confidence grew daily.

Just as his training was nearing the end, he received word his father was dying. Immediately he went to the base commander. "Sir,

I have received word my father is dying. I request permission to see
to his burial arrangements."

"Permission granted. Honoring the dead is important. Take what
time you need, and you may use one of the horses to speed your
journey. Your training will resume when you return."

Titus saluted and walked out. He had already put together what
he would need for the trip home. He picked up his bundle and
walked to the stables for a horse. This would be the longest ride he
had ever taken.

He arrived at his father's home just before he died. There was a
small uproar when he rode through the village nearby. His appear-
ance was certainly news worthy! There had never been a centurion
in the village before. Titus had not been home since he left for the
army some years before. There still were some people that remembered him and many had heard his father talk about him. Now he
appeared dressed as a centurion and on a horse. As he dismounted
in front of his father's home, his sister, Livia, ran out of the house
and threw her arms around him. She began crying hysterically. "Oh,
Titus, I am so glad to see you. I didn't know if you would come or
not. Father is dying. I have been taking care of him the best I could
for the last month." She paused as if she was searching for a word,
"And Titus, after father is dead, I don't know where to go."

"We'll talk later about your future. Right now, take me to father."

Titus found his father's eyes closed and his breathing slow and
weak. His eyes opened when Titus began talking to him. "I'm here,
father, and I will be with you as long as necessary. You rest, and then
we will talk when you feel stronger." His father closed his eyes and
smiled as Titus sat down at his bedside.

Friends and neighbors began arriving at the house. News of
Titus' arrival had traveled fast. Livia said, "Titus, people are gathering in front of our house." Titus went outside to greet them while
his sister stayed at her father's bedside. In a very short time, Livia

came out and said, "Father is dead. He was just looking toward the ceiling as if he expected to see something."

They all rushed inside. Titus kissed his father and closed his eyes. The lamentations began. Titus and his sister washed their father's body and dressed him in his only toga. Livia said to Titus, "The senator's family has given us permission to bury our father in the senator's tomb."

After all their friends and neighbors had taken part in the lamentations, Titus and Livia wrapped their father's body in a cloth and finished preparing him for burial. The closest friends carried his body to the senator's tomb where they laid it in an open space and burned incense to the gods. The tomb was closed, and the burial party returned to the village. Titus and Livia walked home without any conversation.

That night Titus asked Livia, "I know we do not have any relatives that you could stay with, but do you have any close friends you could stay with if I paid them?"

"I don't know of anyone that would be willing to do that," She replied. There was silence.

"We will talk more in the morning. Try to sleep now."

Titus spent a restless night. What to do about his sister occupied his mind. He did not know if she had ever been freed; if not, would it matter? He could not return to the vineyard and replace his father. He had an obligation to the military. On the other hand, he could not just walk away and leave his sister with no place to live. She had taken care of him when he was a child. Now it was his turn to take care of her.

It seemed his only choice was to take her with him. He would ask her in the morning if she had been freed. If not, then he would buy her. But there was still a problem. If she goes with me, she cannot stay on base. Where could she stay? There were so many questions. He had to work something out.

The next morning Titus said, "Livia, was father successful in getting you freed?"

"Yes, he did, just before he got sick."

"So, you would be free to leave here and go with me."

"Yes, I suppose."

"Livia, you need to know the army is my life and right now I am in training, yet I am taking you with me. Don't be upset or start worrying. No matter where I am assigned, you will go with me. So, get your clothes and whatever else you want to take. We will leave as soon as you are ready."

Livia thought to herself, "I'm not sure I want to do this; yet what choice do I have?" She thought for a few minutes and then replied, "All right."

She did not have much to take - just her clothes and a few things that were her mother's, given to her by her father. Titus tied her belongings on the horse. Then the two of them started walking away, leading the horse. It would be a long two-day walk.

They had not gone very far, when Livia turned and looked back to the only home she had known, except for the few months she had been married. Titus could sense her concern. He took her hand and said, "It will be different for you from now on, but I will provide for you and protect you." All the way back, Titus thought, "Where can I find lodging for Livia?"

As darkness approach the first night, Titus said to Livia, "We will find an inn for the night."

"Thank you, Titus, I have never walked so far in my life."

Good fortune was with them because the inn had few guests that night and they secured a place to sleep that provided some privacy. Yet Livia was uncomfortable, "Titus, I have never slept any place but the home I lived in. Here, there are other people nearby. I don't think I can sleep."

"I know this is all new to you, but it will be alright. No one will bother you; I'll make certain of that. And you are tired; you will soon be asleep."

Titus' words helped but Livia still didn't think she would be able to sleep in a room with strangers. However, within minutes her eyelids became heavy, and she was sound asleep. Titus on the other hand slept only in brief periods of time. Any noise or movement brought him to alertness.

The next day, they arose early and continued their journey. It was late afternoon before they finally arrived at the training castrum.

Titus told Livia to wait outside the building while he reported to the Legate.

Titus announced, "Sir, I have returned and am ready to resume my training. But I do have a problem that I need help to resolve."

"What is your problem?"

"I have a sister who has no place to go now that our father is dead. I am her only relative. I brought her back with me."

Titus immediately had the Legate's full attention. He said, "Well, you know she cannot stay on the base with you."

"I know that, sir. I was in hopes you might have a suggestion as to where she might stay. I would be willing to pay someone, if it is not too much."

"I don't know of any place. Housing young women is not part of my responsibilities."

"I know that, but I want to stay in the army, and I can't just tell her to go. She is dependent on me and doesn't have any other source for food and shelter. Please sir, help me."

The commander looked at Titus for a long time without saying anything. Finally, he said, "I will ask my wife tonight. Maybe she knows of someplace. In the meantime, your sister can stay in the guest quarters, but only for a few days. Be sure to tell her not to go walking around the camp."

"Thank you, sir!"

Titus went out and took Livia' hands and said, "Livia, you will be alone for a few days, but do not be afraid. You will have a room for yourself this time. No one will bother you. We just need some time to work things out. You will be staying in the guest quarters. I will come for you as soon as possible."

A reluctant Livia was escorted to the guest quarters. Titus arranged for meals to be delivered to his sister, then he went to his quarters.

Two days later the commander called for Titus Cornelius. "Can your sister cook and keep a household?"

"Yes sir, she is quite capable."

"Good, I have a solution to your problem. Tribune Magnus' wife is very ill, and he needs someone to cook and care for her. They have a daughter, but she is not old enough to be of much help. In return for helping them, they will allow your sister to stay in their home at no cost to you."

Titus was relieved. Now he could concentrate on his training.

"Thank you, sir!" He immediately went to tell Livia. "Livia, I have good news. You are going to stay with a tribune and his wife who is ill. In return for caring for her and keeping house for them, you may stay in their home at no cost. When my training is over, I will take you with me wherever I go."

Livia was having trouble adjusting to this new life. She had already been isolated for two days. Now she was to live with someone she had never met. She told Titus how she felt. He did his best to console her. Finally, she said, "Alright, this seems to be my only choice. So, I will try to make the best of it."

"We will be back together as soon as possible."

Titus resumed his study of battle tactics. He also learned how to lead men in mock battles and what formations to use at the appropriate times. He was even able to practice the formations with live soldiers.

The one event he had hoped he might avoid attending was the commander's banquet, but that was impossible. He was informed of the date and time. Titus dreaded attending this event. He thought to himself, "Well, at least the problem of a female companion has been solved." That evening he dressed in his best toga and went to get Livia. He had bought Livia a new stola made with two different colors and new slippers. He had never thought about the need for a palla which would complete her outfit. Fortunately, Livia had one that the Tribune Magnus' wife had given her. It would complete her outfit. She was so thrilled to get something new, she would have agreed to anything Titus asked.

The banquet was an affair that overwhelmed Titus. Livia felt very uncomfortable. Many military men with female guests and a very few civilians were there. Military protocol was in place prior to and during the meal. There was more food and wine available than people could consume and food he had never seen before. The evening started very formally, but after the meal when the music began playing the atmosphere gradually changed. Soon, there was an atmosphere of drunkenness and impropriety. Livia felt even more uncomfortable and did not want to participate in some of the things taking place. Nor did Titus want to subject his sister to this environment. They left at the first opportunity.

Titus had very few training requirements to complete. They were mostly fill-in activities while he waited on an assignment. Three months later he was assigned to the Italian legion which was led by tribune Arbelardus.

V

Reunion

Titus informed Livia that his training was over, and he had his assignment. They would be moving to Naples. She asked, "How far is that from where father lived?"

"Father's house was north of Rome a half day's journey and Naples is south of Rome about a five-day journey."

"I was in hopes of going back to see our old home."

"I'm sorry, I doubt if that will be possible. However, where we are going is near the seacoast which should be nice."

"I will look forward to that. When will we leave?"

"In three days. Can you finish what you need to do and be ready by then?"

"Tribune Magnus' wife is much better. I don't think I am needed there any longer. They were very nice to me but I am looking forward to living again with you, Titus. I will be ready. Do you know where we will live when we get to Naples?"

"There should be some living quarters available or possibly we could find a house. We'll just have to wait and see."

Livia wondered about living near the sea. She had lived where the only water was a river. How close would they be? Could she walk to the shore and dip her feet in the water? She was excited at the thought of living by the sea. "Oh, Titus, it would be so nice if we lived on the seashore. Do you think that would be possible?"

"I doubt it, but maybe we can go to the seashore when I'm not on duty."

The journey to Naples was uneventful. It was a two day walk so only one night in an inn was necessary. Livia remembered her previous experience of sleeping in an inn. She was not as fearful this time but was still uncomfortable.

With only their clothing and a few personal items there was little to hinder their travel. As they approached the city, Titus said, "Livia, we are almost to Naples. First, I must check in at the castrum. Hopefully that will not take very long. After that we will hunt for a place to live."

They reached the castrum before the city. Titus asked the sentry where the legion tribune could be found. After getting directions, he went to report. "Sir, Titus Cornelius; I have completed training for centurions and have been assigned to your legion. I am reporting to you for duty assignment."

Arbelardus, the legion tribune, replied, "Welcome Cornelius, I have been expecting you. Will you be living in quarters here, or do you prefer living off the castrum?"

"Sir, my sister is in my charge, she is with me so I will need living arrangements off the castrum. Do you have any suggestion as to where living quarters might be available?"

"I don't, but see the actarius. He may have some information that would be helpful to you. Take two days to arrange for your living quarters and get settled in, then report back to me for assignment."

"Yes, sir."

The actarius knew of two different places that were available. He gave directions to both. Titus and Livia left to examine both places. They were thinking that this might be their home for the foreseeable future. It would be good to have some permanency.

Both places were better than where they had lived with their father. Both had a shrine for making sacrifices to the gods, but one could be called a small domus. That was the one they selected because they felt it would satisfy their need for separate privacy and daily living. Plus, it was designed so that inside cooking could be done. Titus discussed the cost with the owner but having never negotiated prices on anything, he was not helping himself. The owner realized this, yet did not want to take advantage of him because he was a centurion.

The owner asked Titus, "You have not done very much bartering, have you?"

"No, I haven't."

"You gave up too quickly in discussing a cost to rent; in the future take your time. You might even walk away. You will get a better price."

"I'll remember that advice."

Livia and Titus walked through their new home questioning what they should do next. Livia told Titus, "I'm grateful that some furniture is already here, but we will need some things." As she walked, she made mental notes on what they still might need. Titus was no help. After they had discovered what was already in place, Livia said, "We need to buy some cooking utensils if I am to cook, and we need food. The furniture can wait a day or two."

Titus added, "All right, we will buy furniture later but we must get a bed for you. I'll take the one that is already here. What about a kitchen table for food preparation?"

"For now, I think there is adequate space to prepare meals."

They put away their belongings and began exploring the nearby area. The first thing they found was a public fountain not very far from their new home. Now they knew where to get water. Next, they located the nearest marketplace where food could be purchased. There were shops for other items such as cooking utensils and household needs. The market was within a short walk from the place they had just rented.

"Titus, I think this will be a good place to live."

They purchased food and a few other necessities. This gave Titus the opportunity to practice what he had learned about bartering with pleasing results. Then they walked back to their new home with their arms full. "Livia, we can buy more on another day."

Livia busied herself putting food away and arranging household items where she wanted them while Titus left again, going in search of a bed. Before daylight was gone, he returned with two men carrying a new bed. The day had been successful.

The next day Titus reported back for duty. Arbelardus was surprised. "I didn't expect you until tomorrow. You are anxious. That is good. I am assigning you to the sixth cohort. Emericus is the senior centurion in that cohort. You will report to him. The centuria I am assigning to you is composed of mostly inexperienced legionaries who need additional training. Can you do that?"

"Yes, sir, I am sure I can to that." After a pause, Titus continued, "Sir, I have been told, I could choose my optio. Is that correct?"

"After you get more familiar with all the legionaries in your group, you can choose whomever you want for your optio."

"If I can choose whomever I want, I already know who that is."

"Do you know some of the men here?"

"No, sir, but if I can choose anyone, there is a legionnaire in Germanicus's command by the name of Primus Constant. That is the man I want to have as my optio."

This was an unusual request. Arbelardus looked Titus Cornelius over from head to foot. He thought to himself, "Here is this new man almost demanding something that will cause me more work. Why should I do it?" After a long silent pause, he decided to pursue this request.

"You obviously know this man, so I won't question that, but you must realize this is unusual. A new optio normally comes from the centuria he was in. Not only would I have to request this, Germanicus would have to agree to transfer him here." Arbelardus paused again, expecting Titus to say something. When he didn't, Arbelardus continued, "How strongly do you feel about this man?"

"Very strongly, sir. He fought beside me in the German campaign. He is an excellent soldier and he will be of great help in training inexperienced men."

Arbelardus thought, it is obvious this man is determined, and, maybe the man he wants could make the centuria better. It would provide two leaders with wartime experience that would be a good example for the younger men." After a few moments of silence, he said, "All right, I will contact Germanicus. If he agrees, I will as well."

"Thank you, sir. You will not be sorry."

"I may not be sorry, but will it be worth the trouble?"

"Sir, I am certain you will find it worth any trouble it may cause."

"Alright, go find Emericus and report to him."

Titus located Emericus and introduced himself. "Sir, Titus Cornelius reporting. I was told the men I am going to command are in need of addition training."

Emericus said, "That is true. Can you do that?"

"Yes" was all Titus said.

"You are taking charge of the sixth centuria."

Emericus was at least 10 years older than Titus. His hair was white and his face was lined. Yet he stood straight as an arrow. He was a classic example of a Roman centurion. The army was his whole life. He would remain in it until he died.

Emericus was friendly enough but totally military. He said, "Tomorrow at the ninth hour there will be a meeting of all the centurions in my cohort. You will meet all of them then. Until then, let's talk awhile so I can get to know you. Later, I'll call together your centuria. If you want to address them, you may."

"Sir, if it's all right with you, I would like to meet with the decani first."

"Smart thinking. I will call them together rather than the entire centuria."

Emericus, having only a sketchy knowledge of Titus asked, "I understand you fought in the Germanic campaign."

Titus answered, "Yes, I did."

Emericus waited, thinking Titus would elaborate, but when he didn't, he asked Titus everything from where he was born to which god did he feel was the strongest. After Emericus was satisfied, Titus had the opportunity ask some questions, which were few. Titus was anxious to meet the decani. Emericus began to sense this and brought the interview to a close. He ended it by saying, "It will take an hour or so to free the decani up, so why don't you walk around the castrum and get familiar with where everything is located."

After touring the castrum, Titus returned and found the decani waiting. When Emericus informed them that Titus would be their centurion all eyes turned to him. Titus waited a moment for them to look him over and then began to speak, looking into the eyes of each man. He said, "You will find me demanding, but fair. I will have no favorites. What I will expect from you is, first, discipline, which should be nothing new. The second, an attitude displaying that our centuria is the best in this cohort. That will take work and effort. We will march more and practice more than any other centuria. I was told the legionaries have no experience in battle. Have any of you been in a battle?" Two responded with a yes.

"That is a help. I want the two of you to tell the others about your experiences and what they can expect in a battle. If you are wondering about me, I have had experience in the German campaign. War is what we must be prepared for first. Why else is an army needed? Until such a time comes, we will accomplish whatever task is assigned to us. If a war should come, we will be prepared to stand until victory is achieved. As for daily regimentation, I will talk more about assignments and daily training later. Are there any questions you want to ask me?"

Emericus was surprised by Titus' offer to answer their questions. He had never known a centurion to expose himself to his subordinates. The decani were surprised as well. They looked at one another then shook their heads, no.

"That is all for now."

After the decani left, they started talking about their new centurion. One said, 'He seems different from past centurions I have served under." There was agreement from all. Another said, "I have never been told that I can ask a centurion anything."

When the men were gone, Emericus asked, "You're allowing your subordinates to question you is very unusual, Cornelius. I can't help but wonder why."

Titus answered, "There were times when I was a decanus that I wanted to ask what was going on, or about something that concerned me and I knew that a question would not be well received. I want these men to feel free to ask me a question. If it is inappropriate, I'll tell them so. Giving them the knowledge that they can ask, may be unusual but I think it will make the men more loyal and willing to respond to commands."

"I don't know about that. I'll be watching to see what happens."

Since Titus' centuria was inexperienced, they were not assigned a road building project, which allowed Titus the opportunity to mold his men into a unified body and a formidable fighting power.

Marching and mock battles filled the days to come in a dull and repetitive manner. When Titus thought his men were becoming bored with the mock battles, he told them, "We will do the exercises over and over until how to fight becomes a habit. In a battle you have to rely on your reactions. You don't have time to think."

One uplifting moment occurred two weeks after Titus requested Primus for his optio. When Primus Constant walked into the room to report, there stood Titus! The meeting was a surprise to both. Titus had not been informed that his request had been granted, and Primus had not known it was Titus he was to report to. Primus just thought he was being reassigned. When he saw Titus, his mouth dropped open and he exclaimed, "I don't believe it!" Both smiled and clasped arms. It was a heartfelt reunion.

Primus spoke first, "You! I had no idea I was reporting to you, Titus. It is good to see you. So, you are truly a centurion now. I never doubted you would become something great. Hopefully we can still be friends as much as possible, with our difference in rank. Titus, I promise never to abuse our friendship."

Titus grabbed Primus by his shoulders and said, "My friend. I requested you for my optio."

"What? I am not on that level and don't know how to fulfill all the duties of an optio."

"That is not true. You have been in the army for several years and have watched optios enough to know everything they do."

"I don't know about that, Titus."

"Well, I do, so you are now an optio. If there is something you do not know, I am sure you will quickly find answers."

"I still have some problems. I don't have the money to buy the required helmet and staff. Another thing, I have never worn chest armor; I don't know if I can and I'm not sure about switching arms to fight."

"Primus, you will receive an increase in pay that will be more than enough to buy what you need. As for the chest armor, if you don't want to wear it, don't buy it."

"All I can say is, I'll do my best. May I say, it is great to be back with you."

"Primus, all this can wait until tomorrow. Tonight, we drink and talk as friends."

Primus went home with Titus and met Livia. "Primus, Livia is my sister. She has lived with me since our father died." She fixed a meal and left them. She could tell they were old friends who had not seen one another for some time. Livia knew they would want to talk and she would not fit into their conversations.

After eating, Titus handed Primus a container of wine and got another for himself. Primus said, "I remember the first night of our basic training. I had learned you could read and write. I told you then you would not remain a foot soldier."

"I had forgotten that. It just proves how smart you are. You're a prophet." Both laughed.

Memories were relived and many were laughed about. Events that had occurred in their lives and changes in their lives were shared. It was late when they clasped arms again and Primus left.

Primus quickly filled the void of a missing optio. It was no surprise that Primus accomplished his new assigned duties from the first day. Titus felt that being reunited with Primus was uplifting. But all too soon the days returned to being dull and uneventful. He knew he must be patient, for this quiet time would give Primus a chance to grow in his new role of optio.

This was a good, peaceful period for the empire, but a boring time for the army. Titus knew his men were tired of daily marches and mock battles. He was growing tired of them, too.

So, he went to Emericus, "I thank you for the opportunity to work with my men without extra assignments. It gave me time to mold the men into a formidable unit. They are now ready for any possible battle. But there are not any battles to fight, so, they are available for any projects you would care to assign."

"Good, Cornelius. I am sure they are. I have been watching your centuria and am pleased with what I see. However, there are no open assignments. There are only some road repairs in the local area that I could assign you."

"We will take them. Hopefully a work project should give my men an opportunity to bond. If nothing else it will give them something to occupy their minds."

"Very well. There are two road repairs that need to be made. I will assign both of them to your centuria."

The next day the sixth centuria marched out to repair a road north of the city. They were led by a proud centurion with a beaming optio bringing up the rear.

VI

Marriage

At home one evening, Titus sat watching the sun go down. He had the look of loneliness about him. Livia sat down with him and said, "Titus, have you ever thought about marriage?"

Titus was surprised at the question. Marriage was a subject that had never entered his mind. "Marriage? Why would I want to get married? I am a soldier and marriage is not encouraged."

"A wife can provide a female companionship that is different from the companionship I provide."

"I don't agree. You are a good companion."

"Thank you, but I know you feel the need of a woman from time to time. As your sister, I cannot fill those needs for you."

"There are ways to satisfy those needs without a wife."

"I realize that, but don't you think you should have a legitimate heir to carry on our family name?"

Titus looked at Livia but said nothing. An heir? He had never considered an heir. Why would he want an heir? He did not answer the question. He just got up and went back inside. That night he laid awake thinking about what his sister had said. Morning did not bring relief.

In his mind a voice said, "All I have thought about these last few years is the army. That is my whole life. I don't have time for anything else. Marriage? How ridiculous. A legitimate heir? I have never thought about having a son."

So went the day. Titus struggled to control his mind. "Why can't I forget about marriage?"

Night came again and this time a restful sleep washed over him. However, just before the sun came up, his eyes popped open. He rolled over, then rolled back. Suddenly he sat up, "Now, when I think about it, I like the thought of having a son."

He couldn't quit thinking about it. He began to wonder, "Why am I having these thoughts? I am too old for this sort of thinking. I should have married five years ago if the gods wanted me to marry. Besides, I don't have permission to marry and I don't plan on seeking permission."

As the day progressed, the words, marriage – wife – son, kept going in and out of his mind. "I have got to get my mind on something else." He saw Primus and asked him, "Primus, did you ever think about getting married?"

"I have never thought about it. Why, are you planning to marry someone?"

"Not really, but I have been thinking about having a son; a legitimate one."

"If you are serious, you need permission to marry you know."

"Yes, I know. I see other officers that are married, so I don't think it is anything more than a formality."

"You have someone in mind?"

"No. To be honest, I have never considered a wife, and I know all the women our age are married or widowed, and I would want a virgin for a wife. Where do you find a woman like that? I don't even know where to look."

"You sound serious about this marriage thing. Whatever got you started thinking like this?"

"Livia asked me about it a couple of nights ago and I can't get it off my mind. It is silly, isn't it?"

"Are you trying to convince me or yourself?"

"I don't know, I'm just thinking about it."

"Well while you are doing all this thinking, tell me what you think about Germanicus's death."

"I didn't know that he was dead. How did he die?"

"From what I hear, no one knows for certain; some say there are some very suspicious circumstances surrounding his death."

"Primus, are you saying someone killed him?"

"I am only telling you what I was told. There is talk that he made several enemies in the senate who wanted him dead."

"Sounds like you are saying some senators had him killed. I know that has happened before, but Germanicus was admired by many and had a large loyal following. That's just hard for me to believe."

"I agree but there is a lot of talk and it may be just rumors. Yet I wonder."

Titus said, "Politics! I never want to be involved. If what you say is true, it reinforces my point. Sad though, the army lost a great leader."

"I too thought he was a great leader."

After a period of silence, Titus said, "Primus, thanks for getting my mind back where it should be."

"Isn't that what friends do?"

Some days and nights the idea of a wife would escape from Titus' subconscious to his conscious mind. He began to notice women more. He paid more attention to what they did or said, especially Livia since she was with him more than any other woman.

He began to think, "If I were really serious about getting married, where would I find a marriageable woman?" But then he would immediately chastise himself. "I've got to get my mind off this marriage thing. There are other things to think about."

Titus had converted the spoils he had accumulated in Germanic war into cash, and his present income provided excess money. He wanted to protect and invest this extra money but didn't know where or how. Since he had no experience in financial matters, he decided to see a banker.

As Titus was on his way to see a banker that had been recommended to him, a very pretty young woman literally ran into him. She was coming out of the banker's office as he was going in. She was not looking in the same direction as she was walking and walked into Titus. The lady said nothing, she just stepped aside and continued.

Normally a Roman male would have growled at her, brushed her aside, and continued on his way. However, Titus was captivated by her looks. He stopped, said nothing, and turned to watch her walk away. She was tall for a woman and had an hourglass figure with black shiny hair. He was captivated by her. He asked a passerby who the young lady was. He was told, "The banker's daughter."

Titus entered the building and met Robertus, the banker. He told him that he wanted to invest some money. The banker agreed to invest his money for a small commission. In the days that followed, Titus kept thinking about the woman he had bumped into that day. He decided to go back to see the banker on the pretext of seeing how his money was doing, and then he could casually ask about his daughter.

After asking a financial question or two, the opportunity presented itself. Titus said, "I may have met your daughter. How is she?

Robertus asked, "Which daughter?"

Titus didn't know how to answer him. He thought, I have already lied and now I don't know what to say. I had better just tell the truth. He said, "The first time I came to see you, I ran into a woman who was coming out of this building. I was told she was your daughter." The banker's eyes rolled, "That one! I have married two other daughters, they were never any trouble, but this one is different. She has a mind of her own. She refused the husband I picked for her. I don't think I'll ever be rid of her."

Titus began to have second thoughts about her. When he returned home, he said to Livia, "I asked the banker about his daughter. She is a pretty young lady. Her father said she was not married and he did not think she would ever get married. He had picked out a man for her to marry, but she refused. I have never heard of a daughter going against her father. Don't you find her attitude strange?"

"I am surprised you asked a question concerning a woman. But in answer to your question, yes and no. I know that fathers decide who their girls are to marry, but if she had a reason, I can understand her refusal."

"Well, I can't. She must be bullheaded and a trouble maker."

"Titus, you are forming an opinion without knowing everything. She may have learned something about that man that her father did not know about, but she could not bring herself to tell him."

"Why wouldn't she tell her father what she learned?"

"Maybe he was a business partner or a special friend, and she knew her father would be devastated by the information. She may have been thinking more about his feelings than her own. There could be some other reason as well, so don't be quick to condemn her."

Titus, wanting to get his mind on something else, dropped the subject and began talking about the good relationship that existed with his men. Livia listened but could not have cared less.

The following morning Titus said to Livia, "After considering what you said yesterday, I believe I was wrong about this woman. I want to meet her. You are the only family I have, so would you go with me to meet the banker and his daughter?"

"Are you serious? Of course, I will go with you, but I am surprised. What made you change your mind?"

"You're the one that said I should get married. Well, this lady is very pretty, and she appears to be strong. That, plus what you said about her thinking more about her father than herself. That struck me as something a mother would do. I like that trait."

As was the custom, arrangements were made for the meeting of the two families. Things did not start well. The banker's daughter, Drusilla, felt she was forced into this meeting and looked holes through Titus in his military toga. Meanwhile, Titus looked her over with an approving eye. Robertus was quick to notice. He began to perk up thinking this may be his last chance to get rid of his youngest daughter who had defied his choice for her husband. Livia wondered about Drusilla's attitude, but just smiled and kept her thoughts to herself.

By the end of the evening, things softened enough that another meeting was arranged. Robertus suggested Titus and Livia come back for an evening meal and they agreed. As they left Titus asked Livia, "Drusilla is much younger than I. Do you think there might be too much difference in our ages?"

"I don't think age will make any difference if the two of you are compatible."

"I thought that age might be a be a factor in a relationship, but you are saying it doesn't have to be. That is reassuring to me."

Things went a little smoother the second time. Titus sensed Drusilla's attitude had improved. Had sharing a meal set a friendlier tone? He wondered but was pleased.

After dinner the two of them engaged in some conversation. He learned she was 21, rather old for an unmarried female. Drusilla, knowing very little about the military, learned Titus was a centurion, which to her only meant he was not a common soldier. After Titus and Livia had left, she learned that a centurion had social status so she began to be impressed.

The evening had gone smoothly enough for a third get-together to be arranged. This time Drusilla was more congenial. Still, Titus questioned if she had changed on her own, or if her father had convinced her to change.

He decided it did not matter. The fact that her attitude had improved was all that was important. They began to spend more time together. Occasionally Titus started bringing small gifts such as flowers or jewelry.

Both Drusilla and Titus discovered they liked many of the same things. They enjoyed one another's company but a romantic love was missing. Both began to think about marriage from a self-serving point of view. Drusilla thought a marriage with Titus would provide her a respectable social position, security, and freedom from her father's nagging. From Titus' viewpoint, marriage would provide a means to having a legitimate son. Besides, Drusilla was a pretty woman who was pleasant to be around. The two felt they had gained a new friend more than a marriage partner.

They continued to spend time together. They went to the hippodrome to watch horse races. Sometimes they just went for a walk. Drusilla was more willing to talk about her past than Titus was of his. Fortunately, that did not seem to bother her.

Finally, the subject of marriage surfaced and plans for a wedding were arranged. Drusilla began to sew her wedding garments as was the custom, while Titus went to Arbelardus to ask for permission to marry. After permission was granted, a date was set. Drusilla's father, Robertus was so thrilled, he presented Titus with a dowry of two slaves and a hectare of land.

Titus did not want to accept the dowry and said so, but Robertus said, "It is the custom. Besides, one of the slaves is a female that Drusilla has known since she was a baby and feels very close to. She will be pleased. The other slave is Coto. He is very trustworthy and you will find him very helpful to you. As for the land, it will provide a place for you to go when you retire from the army." When Titus saw he did not have a choice in the matter, he said, "Thank you."

The day before the wedding, Titus told Livia, "You will always have a home with me, and I feel certain you and Drusilla will not have a problem living in the same house."

Livia replied, "Thank you, Titus. I was not sure what was going to happen to me after your marriage. I did make arrangements to be gone tomorrow night and the next night. I will stay with a neighbor I have made friends with. Titus, I promise not to cause any problems in your marriage."

While the two of them ended the day reminiscing. Drusilla was giving all of her childhood belongings to her family members and thanking her parents for what they had done for her.

The next morning Drusilla bathed, paid special attention to her hair, and then put on the wedding dress that she had made. Lastly, she covered her head with a veil and a floral wreath.

Titus selected a young boy to lead the bridal party to Drusilla's house. There, Drusilla came out with her family to join the procession to Titus' house. The boy lit a special torch and led the way. As they passed one of Titus's neighbors, Drusilla gave him a copper coin to signify she would be staying in the neighborhood. Once they arrived at Titus' house, the torch was extinguished and the ashes given to those in the party. A new, smaller torch was lit from the fire in the groom's house. The small torch and some water were given to the bride as was the custom.

Titus went in first. Then the bride's attendants lifted her over the threshold where she said, "Titus, are you there? I am Drusilla, your wife."

Titus answered, "I am here. Make your home with me."

As many as possible then came inside. Titus and Drusilla made a bridal sacrifice to the goddess, Juno. Then they clasped hands and raised them high. At that point they were considered married, a cheer was made and congratulations were given. Afterwards everyone left the newlyweds.

The next day Titus gave a huge dinner party where the wine flowed freely. Friends of both wished the newlyweds well. Drusilla's friends outnumbered Titus' friends who were all military. The most joyful person at the festivities was Drusilla's father, Robertus.

Married life agreed with Titus. His demeanor softened, and a fondness grew between him and Drusilla. He also discovered that Coto was very helpful, so he kept Coto with him most of the time, even when he was at the castrum.

Livia continued living with the newlyweds but always kept a proper distance.

Nine months after their marriage, a son was born. Livia assisted in the birth. She took the baby boy to Titus. He took one look and the baby started crying. Titus jumped backwards saying, "I never touched him! He must not like me."

"Nonsense, Titus. His eyes are not developed enough even to see you clearly. He may be just hungry. Babies cry when they are hungry."

Titus continued to back away. "You take care of him. Men don't take care of babies."

"I will. Now, you should go in to see Drusilla"

Titus never questioned Livia. He never displayed the masculine superiority of a Roman man with his sister. Now, he felt he was in foreign territory. He walked into the next room where Drusilla was laying. "How do you feel?" he asked as he knelt beside her.

"Weak and tired but I'll be all right. Have you seen the baby?"

He was glad Drusilla was asking a question. "Yes. He cried when he saw me." Titus answered.

"That is a baby's nature. You will hear him cry several times in the days to come."

"What do we call him?

"Have you thought about a name?"

Titus had not even considered a name, but he did not want to tell Drusilla that. "I don't have a favorite. Do you have a suggestion?"

"What do you think of the name, Alexius?"

"That is a good name, Drusilla. Let's name him, Alexius."

Livia cared for both the baby and Drusilla until Drusilla recovered from the birth. The two could not have bonded more if they had been sisters.

At home, Titus seemed indifferent where the baby was involved. He was stiff and awkward around the baby. He did not know what to do with a baby. When he was asked if he would like to hold Alexius, he refused for fear of breaking him. But away from his home, when he had other men around him, his pride exploded. He talked with Primus and anyone else near him about his son. Finally, Primus cautioned Titus he was overdoing it.

Titus' joy was interrupted six months after Alexis' birth by an announcement that had only been rumors until now. Some of the legion was to be reassigned to Judea as replacements for men returning to Italia.

The women learned of the news about as soon as the men.

In the evening when Titus came home, Drusilla had so many questions that she never gave Titus a chance to speak. "Are you going to go? When would you go? Where is Judea? Is that where you would go? Will I go with you?" Livia was anxiously listening.

When Drusilla realized she wasn't giving Titus a chance to answer, she stopped. Titus looked at both of them and said, "Drusilla and you, too, Livia, the only question I can answer is, Judea is on the eastern end of the Mediterranean Sea. Your other questions I should be able to answer tomorrow. All the centurions are to attend a briefing in the morning about a deployment. I should know then if I am to go or stay."

VII

Judea

All the centurions were anxiously awaiting the news concerning their possible transfer to another country and they reported early for the briefing. Rumors buzzed throughout the room.

Everything went quiet when Tribune Arbelardus entered right on time. He began, "I know you're all eager to find out who is going and as well the destination. The destination is Caesarea, Judea. Only three centuriae will be going. They will be selected by Emericus since they are to come from his cohort. The rest of his cohort will remain here unless there is an urgent need for them to go. If that should occur, they must be prepared to leave immediately. The three centuriae that are leaving will be going in three days. I believe you already know this is a rotation assignment. They will be replacing three centuriae that are returning to Italia. Those that go can expect to stay for three years, unless conditions there should change, or there is an urgent need for them someplace else. That is all for now. Everyone except Emericus and his centurions are dismissed."

There was a rumble of voices as most of the group left. When everything quieted down, the seven men that were left with Arbelardus moved together. Emericus asked, "Should our optiones be here?"

"No, you can pass the information on to them and your legionaries. I am just going to discuss the mission with you. You may ask a question if something is not clear."

Without waiting, Titus asked, "Will it be possible for families to go?"

Arbelardus was not anticipating this question because he didn't think any of them had a wife. Then he remembered Cornelius had asked about available housing. He looked straight at Titus and responded, "This is not an order, but I think it best if you all go alone at this time. After you arrive in Judea, evaluate the country and conditions. Then make your decision about moving your family. If you want to move your family, we will make arrangements for their shipboard passage. If you decide your family would be safer and better off in Italia, they will have the army's protection while you are gone."

"Thank you, sir; you make a good point."

Arbelardus asked, "Emericus, I know this is asking you to make a decision on short notice, but do you know which centuriae out of your cohort should go?"

Emericus looked each of the other centurions in the eye and thought for a moment. "Yes, sir, I will go with the first, Marcus will go with the third, and Cornelius will go with the sixth."

"All right. Those three centuriae will sail to Caesarea where our main headquarters in Judea is located. One centuria is to go on to Jerusalem. I think that should be Marcus' centuria. The other two are to stay in Caesarea for the present time.

"There is also a small castrum at Capernaum. But that centuria is staying in place because centurion Ludo requested a permanent assignment there. Why anyone would want to stay in Judea rather than return to Italia is hard to understand, but it is true.

"As for the situation in Judea, there have only been a few minor troubles reported recently; however, there has been some fighting in the past. I don't expect any outbreaks or revolts, but if major problems should develop, send word back and the entire legion will come. I don't foresee you having any problems with the local people."

Marcus asked, "What can you tell us about the people who live there?"

"All I know is they are mostly Jews, and they have a strange religion. They only believe in one god and believe they are a special group of people. I don't know how they justify that idea since we conquered them. They seem peaceful enough, just somewhat unfriendly, and they tend to be uncooperative. Be cautious in your dealings with them. Although they may appear to be trustworthy, they may not be.

"It is a hot dry area so always keep water available. Individual weapons and support equipment are all that you will need to take with you. There is no need to take battle rams or siege equipment. All that is already in place. Now go and prepare your men to march to the sea. You must be ready to depart early the third morning from now."

Titus had mixed emotions. He did not want to be separated from his family, yet there was a thrill of going to another country that stimulated him. He sought Primus and told him they would be leaving and to call the decani together as quickly as possible. By the time they met two hours later, the news had already spread throughout the entire legion.

When the decani was completely assembled, Titus addressed them. "Three days from now, our centuria will depart for Judea. All of us are going. The first and third centuriae are going as well. We will march to the coast and board ships. Then we will sail to Caesarea in Judea where our centuria will be staying. The third centuria will continue on to Jerusalem. Now go tell your men to prepare to leave. They will need to take everything in their possession because we will be there for three years, or possibly longer.

Constant is in charge of packing all support equipment. He will assign a detail of five men to assist him."

One of the decani said to Titus, "I have never been on a boat. What is it like being on a boat?"

Titus smiled, "I don't know. I have never been on a boat either. It will be a new experience for many of us."

"Question, sir, how long will it take to sail to Caesarea?"

"I do not know. I'm sure it will take several days."

After giving instructions for departure and taking care of some daily duties, Titus left for the day. He knew there were two anxious women waiting for him to come home. As soon as he arrived, they began questioning, "Are you going to leave? Will we go with you?"

"Yes and no. I will be leaving three days from now for Judea, but I think it would be best if you two and Alexius stay here for now." Titus sensed their disappointment and concern. He could see the women's lips begin to quiver. He continued, "I don't want to leave without both of you and Alexius, but I don't know what the conditions are where we are going. I don't want to expose my family to any possible danger. After I get there and have a chance to look things over, and, if it seems safe for you to join me, I will send for you."

Drusilla started to say something but Titus held up his hand and said, "I just think it will be better to do it this way because I do not know if the people there are unfriendly or possibly rebellious. I need to verify that it is safe."

Drusilla replied, "What if it is not safe, or what if you don't think we should come? How long might we be separated?"

"I don't want to think about that possibility. But if it does turn out that way, it will be at least three years. It could be longer. The unit we will be replacing has been there for five years." There was silence in the room. Everyone was lost in their own thoughts. Livia said, "I'm cooking lamb. I need to check on it." She walked away.

The evening meal was eaten in silence. That night was a quiet night with Titus and Drusilla holding one another. The next morning Titus left early, knowing the women would still be asleep. He did not want to disturb them. Everyone's emotions were on edge.

Thoughts in Titus' mind bounced from one subject to another. There were many things to attend to if his centuria was to be fully prepared to sail in two days. Yet his heart was heavy with the thought of leaving Drusilla and his son. He knew he had to focus on the move. He was responsible for 92 men. Duty and marriage often conflict.

Arriving at the castrum he found a scurry of activity involving all the men in his centuria. He called together the decani and Primus. "What progress has been made in the preparations?" Primus delivered a complete report. Tents and bedding for the men were being loaded on carts. Additional weaponry for any necessary replacement, was also being prepared for shipment. A two weeks' supply of food and water was being packed. Titus said, "Two weeks of food may not be enough. Add enough for four more days." Other than that, he was satisfied with their reports. When asked about moving heavy equipment, Titus said, "Battle rams and other heavy battle equipment would not be necessary because they were already in place."

On the afternoon before departure, Arbelardus called for Emericus, and the two other centurions to report for their final instructions.

"There is one thing I should tell all of you that could make a difference in your assignment. Augustus is spending most of his time on his estate in Capri and is becoming less involved in government affairs. I would guess we will soon have a new Caesar. I and most other tribunes want no part of politics. Hopefully any possible transfer of power will go smoothly. There have been times when…". His voice trailed away. Arbelardus realized he was becoming political. He paused and took a deep breath.

Then he said, "I, personally, will send word if you need to return for any reason. I will say no more. Now, one task you are to perform after arrival concerns Centurion Ludo in Capernaum. He is staying and wants to do so for the rest of his life. That seems strange to me. Why would anyone not want to come back to Italia? The reports I have received about him state he has become very close to the Jewish people. Maybe he is too close. I am told he has even paid for some building for the god they worship. Emericus, you are to send someone there to find out if Rome's interests are still being upheld by Ludo and if he is capable of performing his duties. Then send word of your findings to me. If there is any problem there, I want it nipped, before it takes root."

In Arbelardus' opinion, Ludo was crazy. He wondered if more needed to be said about Ludo. After a pause he decided, no. He continued, "You will march out at the seventh hour in the morning. The lead ship you will sail on is named Corbito. There are two other ships, but I don't know their names. They will be waiting for you in Naples. Get your men and supplies on board as soon as possible. When the winds and weather are favorable, the ships will sail. If the gods are with you, you should arrive in 12 days or less. That is all. Hail Caesar!" The three men replied in like manner.

The rest of the day was busy with preparations. Titus went home for the last night with his family until fate would bring them together again. Conversation was difficult at the evening meal that night. The women had prepared all the family's favorite foods, but little was eaten. The looming departure had affected everyone's appetite. No one wanted to talk about the next day. The only subject that lasted very long revolved around Alexius.

Later Drusilla and Titus went for a walk. Neither said very much, they just walked. The closeness they shared that evening would be treasured in the weeks and months of separation that lay ahead. They did not realize what a treasure it was at the moment.

Returning home, they retired for the night, but Titus could not sleep. He finally got up quietly and gathered his things. He could not bring himself to wake Drusilla to say goodbye; it would have been too emotional for him.

He did wake up Coto. "Coto, I am leaving you with my family. I want you to watch after them. If it is safe where I am going, I'll send for them. You are to come with them and protect them from any harm."

Coto assured Titus, "Do not worry about your family. I will protect them from all harm."

Titus did not wake anyone else. He checked on his sleeping son, kissed Drusilla lightly on her forehead, then quietly walked out of the house long before sunrise.

At the castrum all the preparations had been made. Emotions were high, and the men were ready. At seven that morning, three centuriae marched out of the castrum. Each centurion led his group of men. There were several people lining the road watching these men march away including Drusilla, little Alexius, and Livia. Titus saw them wave and wanted to rush over to them and embrace all three. But he maintained military protocol and kept his eyes looking forward.

They arrived at the shipping docks three hours later. The Corbito and two other ships were there. By the time they got everything loaded and the men boarded, the sun was low on the horizon. The men had set up tents on deck and settled in for the voyage. The centurions had private cabins. Titus shared his with Primus.

The three centurions met with the three ship captains to report that their loading was complete and they were ready to sail.

The Corbito's captain told them, "We will sail on the midnight tide if the gods agree and winds are favorable." But there was no wind at midnight, so, the three ships remained at the dock. Disappointed men settled in for the rest of the night. They were hoping the ship would sail with the mid-night tide. They had stayed awake to witness the departure from the dock.

Morning came, but the captain did not feel that the day was a good day to sail. In his opinion, the gods and the stars were not aligned for sailing. They would not be leaving. He left the three centurions standing on the Corbito's deck. Emericus's face turned red but there was nothing he could do. The ship's captain was in charge of the sailing.

Almost three hundred men plus the three ships' crews made for crowded conditions. Emericus knew that it was going to be this way for 12 days. He remained quiet for a short period of time while he looked out over the water. He turned and said to Titus and Marcus, "Unless you disagree, let's give the men freedom to leave the ships until sunset. We will be packed on these ships long enough."

Both centurions agreed, and the men were elated. This would be their day of pleasure before sailing. The only problem was many of them came back that evening drunk. Emericus said, "Some of these fellows are going to be sick before we get to the open sea. Make sure they are near the sides of each ship; I don't want to stink up a ship on the first day at sea."

At dawn the next morning, the Corrbito's captain felt that the winds and tide were just right. He announced that the gods were blessing them. He was now ready to leave. At the sixth hour, the sails went up, and the ships pushed away from their moorings. The Corbito glided smoothly away from shore. When they first hit open water, the waves were small and more sails were hoisted. At once the ship began to increase its speed. As the boat reached full open sea, the waves became larger and the ship rolled more. Many of the men were still experiencing the effects of drunkenness, which did not mix with the ship's movement over water. Titus looked around the ship and said to himself, "Emericus was right. There must be a least 25 men hanging over the side of this ship."

By nightfall the sea became calmer and the men improved and were able to settle down. They quickly learned how to exist on an open deck with little space between men.

The fourth day out, a storm developed. As the waves grew larger, the ship began to roll and pitch much more than the first day on the sea. Several men who had escaped through the drunkenness without getting sick, were unable to escape being seasick this time. Titus adjusted to the unstable conditions without any adverse effects. He was concerned about his men and the security of their supplies. He looked for Primus and found he was one of the seasick group. He was leaning over the railing, holding on for dear life and vomiting. Titus chided him saying jokingly, "Got a weak stomach?"

Primus replied, "I don't have a weak stomach. I'm throwing it out there as far as anyone." Titus laughed, which didn't help Primus any. He left Primus and began checking on the men's conditions and the security of their supplies. That evening the winds and sea calmed down. Very few were interested in an evening meal. Everyone was hoping for smooth sailing the rest of the way.

Day after day there was nothing to see but water. Because of the crowded conditions there could be no marching and very little exercising. The men ate little and neither did Titus. He was bored, and he knew the men were as well. To pass time, the legionaries gambled in dice games and there were some wrestling matches arranged. There was nothing else to do but wait.

Primus and Titus would reminisce from time to time. Events from the German campaign were recalled and battles were refought. Humorous stories of heavy drinking brought some smiles, then some shame. On occasion, were the words, "Did we really do that?", expressed by one or the other, followed by laughter.

One morning, Primus asked, "Titus, did you ever wonder if life had a purpose?"

"No, but the purpose of life is living, otherwise you are dead."

"What I meant was, is there something we are supposed to do in our life? Why are we even born? Is there some great power that controls what happens in our lives?"

Titus looked at Primus and said, "Has all this idleness and nothing to see but water got you thinking about such deep subjects?"

"Maybe. With nothing to do I have been thinking about a lot of things. I thought about the difference between us. You grew up as a slave and now you are a centurion, while I grew up a free person but have not improved my status. True, I am an optio, but that is due to your action not anything I did. I am not jealous. I think what has changed for you is your purpose in life. But what is mine? Do I have some purpose? If I do, I don't know what it is."

"Primus, I have never considered my advancement as a purpose in life. But I do believe the gods controlled the events that caused my good fortune. I just don't know if it was just one god, or all the gods were involved. A bigger mystery is why was I chosen?"

"I guess they thought you were deserving, but I think there are things we will never know."

Titus said, "You are right about that." Nothing more was said by either. Both men stood quietly starring out at the water, but Primus' questions seeped through their minds. Titus began to have new questions disturb him. He asks himself is there some great power looking over us? Does this life have a purpose? If it did, what was his purpose? Years later, Titus would recall this conversation and the questions.

After twelve days of looking at nothing but water, the sight of land came into view one morning. The first man to see it, pointed and yelled out "Land!". Then a second man did likewise. Soon everyone on board was cheering. The tents came down, and personal belongings were packed away. The ships followed the coastline south for half a day until a city came into view. Preparations were quickly made to land at Caesarea. A loud roar of, "Finally!" went up from the men as they came alongside the dock.

Disembarking began. No one was happier than Titus. Solid land felt good to every one of them; however, their legs had to re-adjust to walking on a surface that was not moving and rolling. After all the men and equipment had been offloaded and placed on carts, a formation was ordered and accomplished quickly.

The three centuriae marched toward the fortress under the curious eyes of a large contingent of local men. Titus could sense that these people were displeased to see them entering their country. He felt he was viewed as an intruder. It brought back memories of his days in Germanic territories. Fortunately, there were no battles to fight here.

At the fortress a small group of officers came out to greet the arrival of the new legionaries. Emericus saluted and reported to the tribune in charge of the fortress, who told him to use the next two days for his men to recover from the voyage. "Thank you, sir, we will spend the time marching and exercising. We did not have room to maneuver on the ship."

The tribune replied, "Yes, I remember how I felt when I arrived. Come and tell me when your men are ready to assume normal duties. At that time your centuriae will replace the centuriae that have left."

Emericus told Marcus and Titus to dismiss their men to settle in to their quarters. Titus found his quarters very small and simple, less than what a Centurion would have back in Italia. But he corrected his thinking, by asking himself, "Have I grown soft? These quarters are as good as what I lived in as a boy. Why am I comparing them to what I had in Italia?"

That evening Titus and Primus met. They stayed inside of the fortress, not being sure what they might experience out among the local people. They would save that until later. Titus asked Primus if his quarters were adequate. Primus said, "I am quartered with the legionaries. I do have a little more room than they do, but that is all. I have had worse."

"Sorry, but there is nothing I can do for you," replied Titus.

After two days of better food, exercising, marching and getting adjusted to being on land again, Emericus reported back to the tribune. Emericus was told, "Your men will replace the centuriae that left in the patrol rotation schedule. There is a schedule for what towns are to be visited and when. Basically, you will patrol for a week and serve in the fortress for three weeks."

Arrangements were made for Marcus' centuria to leave for Jerusalem with a guide. Emericus said to Marcus, "I know you are capable and will do well. Do not hesitate to send word back if you need help." Marcus left with his centuria the next morning. Emericus and Titus and their centuriae stayed in Caesarea.

Since they had two weeks before their first patrol, Titus and Primus took advantage of their assignment for the next 10 days to get familiar with Caesarea. They located market places and where selected shops were. Every day they ventured out further from the area around the fortress. The first thing Titus noticed was the local people kept their distance from the Romans and their fortress.

Titus found their duties, other than patrols, were the same as in Italia with the exception of guard duty. They were in another country so more emphasis was placed on guard duty than back in Italia. Here guards needed to be more alert and observant for any possible theft or rebellious activity. It did not take long for routines to develop. There were patrol routes to follow, then then a few free days, ending with duty at the fortress. Titus thought time was standing still.

VIII

An Aching Heart

Seven months later, Titus could stand it no longer; he missed his family. It had been too long since he had seen them. He had been in Caesarea long enough to determine that the city was calm and safe. It had been peaceful throughout the entire Judean countryside. He saw no reason not to send for them. He would do it as soon as he returned to the castrum from the rotational patrol he was on.

The first night back Titus wrote a letter to Drusilla, telling her to come with Livia and Alexius as soon as possible. He missed them more than he could put into words. He took the letter to the captain of a supply ship that was headed back to Italia, asking him to take it back to his family near Naples. The captain agreed to take the letter back to Naples and deliver it to the castrum that Titus had left. Titus felt confident that the letter would be passed on to Drusilla. Now all that he could do is wait.

Titus was grateful that it would be three weeks before he was scheduled to lead another patrol. This would allow time to find living quarters for his family. The next morning, he started out to look for a suitable place for his family to live. For several days whenever he had free time, he would walk through the town, looking for an appropriate place his family could call home. He found most of the local people were polite enough but tended to shy away from him. Obtaining information about available housing was difficult. Whenever he found a place that might work for his family, he had trouble locating the owner. Then, when he did, the rental price was outrageous.

He had looked for two weeks without any success. He was becoming frustrated and beginning to worry. His family would expect a place to live when they arrived. Time was running out. He had one week left before he went back on patrol. As he returned to the fortress that evening, he kept telling himself, "It's imperative that I find a suitable place for my family this week."

Shortly after he started the next morning, he was approached by a local man named Fishel. He said, "I have been watching you for the last two weeks, centurion. What or whom are you looking for?" Titus studied him. He didn't know if this man was a threat or not. He didn't know if he should even speak to him or not, but the man did know his language and appeared safe enough. After some hesitancy Titus answered, "I am looking for a place to live. I am thinking about moving my family here."

Fishel asked, "So, you are planning to stay here for a while?"

Titus answered, "Yes, but I can't find any place suitable unless I agree to a price that is higher than I can pay."

"That is because you are not a Jew. Sorry, but true. I might be willing to help you for some financial consideration."

Titus, feeling that he didn't have any choice, asked, "What would you consider an appropriate financial consideration?"

"I would say five denarii might be right, don't you think?"

Surprised at the amount, Titus responded, "Five denarii! That is pay for five days of labor!"

"True, but I can save you much more than that in rent payment. It is up to you; keep looking if you want, but you will not be able to finding anything."

Thinking about his experience of searching on his own, Titus concluded that the man was probably right. He'd not had any luck finding anything on his own. He said, "All right, I'll give you a chance. If you find something I like and at a price I can afford, I will give you five denarii." Fishel said, "Come back to this place tomorrow when the sun is at its highest."

Titus returned to the fortress. As soon as he arrived, he learned a ship had arrived from Italia with a very important passenger by the name Pontius Pilate, who had been appointed Prefect of Judea. Titus was to report for a briefing concerning Pontius Pilate as soon as possible. He ran to the meeting room where the tribune and Emericus were waiting. "Centurion Cornelius, we have been waiting for you. Take care of your personal business after your duties have been fulfilled not before!"

"Yes, sir, I did not think I would be needed on such short notice. I am sorry for any delay I have caused you."

The tribune said, "The reason I have called for you is Pontius Pilate, the new Prefect has arrived. He will represent Caesar's interests in Judea and he will be responsible for order and peace. My orders, which were signed by the Emperor, state we are to respect all of his requests and follow his orders." There was a pause.

"What I say next does not leave this room. I have heard some things about this man. He must have high level friends; otherwise, I wonder if he would have obtained this appointment. We are part of the Imperial Army of Rome, not part of some political group. If he should order us to do anything that conflicts with our military protocol, we will discuss our response before acting. Remember that, Cornelius, if you are given an order by Pontius Pilate that seems questionable. As for now, select twelve men to escort Pilate to Jerusalem when he is ready to move."

Titus asked Primus to lead the detail and together they selected twelve men. Titus instructed Primus to return as soon as Pilate was settled in his quarters.

After one day of rest, Pilate left for Jerusalem. He was beginning his assigned authority with a distaste for Jews. Pilate planned to spend the winter in Jerusalem, and he felt by spring he could establish his control and undermine Jewish customs. He intended to honor Emperor Tiberius by placing a bust of him on the roads into Jerusalem. He arrived in the city late in the afternoon. That night, in the hours of darkness, he had busts of the emperor placed on standards at the city entrances. This, he thought, would show him to be a strong man in control and provide proof of his respect of Tiberius.

When morning came and the busts were discovered, it did not take long for riots to develop in the streets. What Pilate did not know was, not only did the Jews dislike Roman authority, Jewish religious laws forbid the making of images. Marcus quickly dispatched soldiers to restore order, and he sent word to Caesarea of a possible outbreak. Pilate ordered Marcus to herd all the Jews who were demonstrating into the stadium where he addressed them. "The busts of Caesar are there to honor him. They are not going to be removed. Your demonstrating will not change anything. So, if you Jews do not end this riot and return to your homes, I will instruct the soldiers to kill all of you."

They responded by throwing themselves on the ground and baring their throats. Marcus and most of the soldiers with him were astounded. The fact that the Jews would sacrifice their lives rather than defile their laws even touched Pilate. Marcus looked at Pilate and said, "We cannot and will not kill men that have this strong of a belief." Pilate looked at Marcus for a long silent moment, then turned and walked away without saying anything. It was going to be harder than he anticipated to establish his authority. Marcus released the Jews.

The next day the busts were removed and calm returned to the city. When news of peace being re-established, reached Caesarea,

Emericus was relieved. Both he and Titus had prepared to go to Jerusalem in support of Marcus. Now, no reinforcements would be needed. Titus was relieved as well; he could turn his attention back to finding a home.

Unfortunately, Titus never made the meeting with Fishel. Pontius Pilate's arrival followed by his failed plan and the uproar he had caused, resulted in Titus being on an alert status for five days. However, he did get word to Fishel that presently he was unable to meet him, but he was still interested in finding a home, and he would meet him at the earliest time possible. He asked for a suggested place and time to meet as soon as he was relieved.

Fishel complied with the request, and the day after Titus was relieved, the two were able to meet. True to his word, Fishel had found a place for Titus' family to live. It was even nicer than what they had in Italia and was cheaper. The house was located on the south edge of the city. It was a spacious house with a courtyard and surrounded by a wall 1.8 meters high. The owner was a wealthy Jewish merchant whose children were grown and whose wife had died. He had no interest in continuing to live in the house.

When Titus saw the house, he was pleased and thought Drusilla would be as well. He thanked Fishel and paid him five denarii. Finding a home for his family had been more difficult than he had anticipated, but he was pleased with the end result. There was only one day left before patrolling would begin again. Success in finding a home had come none too soon, but now he could relax.

A few days later while he was on patrol, Titus had need of a translator. Not knowing any other options, he sent a messenger to locate Fishel and ask him to translate for him. He agreed to return with the messenger and translate as needed. Titus soon discovered that Fishel was reliable and dependable. He even began serving as a guide on some of Titus' military patrols. Soon Titus began to depend on him. Of course, there was always a charge for Fishel's services.

Days went by slowly as he waited for his family. His heart began to ache. He was sorry he had not paid more attention to his wife and son when he had been with them. He dreamed of putting his arms around Drusilla and holding her close and feeling her warmth. He wondered how much his son had grown. No longer could he ignore how much he actually loved and missed his wife and son. He thought, "My father was right, you never know what you are missing until it isn't there any longer."

His mind raced! "Had they left yet? Where were they right now? How close might they be to Caesarea? Oh, if only my family had the wings of a bird and could fly here!"

He continued to live at the fortress. When duty did not call, he would go to the house Fishel had found for him. On some days he marched out with a contubernium to a village someplace. Other times, Primus would take charge of the patrol. Very rarely did they discover any problems, but when they did, only small corrective action was needed to solve the situation and it was taken immediately.

Meanwhile, Marcus was experiencing conditions that were totally different. The Jews in Jerusalem were very upset again and were reaching the point of rebelling. The problem centered around Emperor Tiberius who was angered when he heard about the resistance Pilate met when he placed the emperor's busts on the roads into Jerusalem and their subsequent removal. Tiberius' anger inflamed the resentment he already had for the Jewish people. In retaliation he planned to set a statue of himself in the temple in Jerusalem. To justify doing so, he began by decreeing he was divine.

Tiberius' next move was to send his legate to Syria and from there, he was to lead a force into Judea and take control of Jerusalem, by force if necessary. As soon as control was established, a large statue of Tiberius was to be placed in the temple. The Jews learned of this plan about the time the legate and his forces arrived in Syria. The monotheistic Jews were not about to let this happen. They were not going to allow the Romans any access to their temple. Opposition plans were formulated. They began amassing weapons and making plans to revolt. When Marcus became aware of what was about to happen, he sent an urgent request for more men to Emericus.

News of the situation in Jerusalem quickly reached Rome. Fortunately, there had been some wiser heads in Rome that knew Tiberius had made a serious mistake when he issued the decree and had talked him out of continuing with his Jerusalem plan before any action had taken place. Word of the change in Tiberius' plans arrived back in Caesarea not long after Marcus' request for help had arrived. Titus was glad Emericus had decided not to depart for Jerusalem until Marcus provided the latest information on the potential revolt. Both Emericus and Titus had their centuriae prepared for the second time and were ready to lead them to Jerusalem. The possibility of warfare filled Titus' thinking, blocking out the arrival of his family.

As soon as this news was received, a fast messenger was dispatched to Jerusalem. The message he carried read, *"Tiberius has rescinded his order to place a statue of himself in the temple. If more soldiers were sent to Jerusalem, it could be interpreted in the wrong way. Share this message with the Jewish authorities and reassure them Roman legions will not support a request to place a statue in the temple. We hope that peace can be maintained."* It was to be delivered to the Jewish leaders.

After this information had spread throughout the city, there was no more talk of a revolt. Marcus was able to report back to Emericus that the threat of a revolt had been averted.

As soon as the threat ended, Titus' mind reverted to concerns for his family. He had no knowledge of where they were presently located and the separation from his family was eating away his heart.

He found himself daydreaming. "If they cannot have the wings of a bird, make me a bird, and I will fly out across the waters to find them. Then I will become the wind and blow the ship along faster."

Titus recalled when he sent the instructions to join him to Drusilla, but he did not know how long it would be before she saw them. He began to calculate how long it would take for her to make arrangements to join him and the travel time to get to Judea.

Actually, the instructions had taken two months to reach them. Another two months went by during which their house was closed up and passage arranged. Finally, household items and what the ladies felt were bare necessities were loaded aboard a ship. Most of this work was accomplished by Coto. After a period of time that Drusilla thought was an eternity, they were on a ship sailing away from Naples. Both women were apprehensive and anxious.

The first night at sea, Drusilla and Livia were looking out over the water at the moon starting to rise into the sky. Drusilla said, "Livia, I want to tell you how my love for Titus has grown from just liking him to fully loving him. When Titus and I married, I liked him and enjoyed being with him but I was not in love with him. I just saw our marriage as a way to escape from my father's continual talk about what he considered my failure to marry. Then when Alexius was born, I felt love for the first time in my life, mostly toward Alexius, yet my feeling toward Titus began to grow. It has grown much stronger since he has been gone. And now, I love Titus from the bottom of my heart. I hope my confessing this to you, doesn't change your opinion of me?"

"No, Drusilla it does not. I suspicioned as much when you married Titus but I didn't say anything. You have been good to him and you are a good mother. The way you felt in the past is not as important as how you feel now. I believe you love him now, that is what matters."

Drusilla continued, "This separation has made me realize just how much I do love him. Since Titus left, I have spent many nights lying in bed searching for him before I would awaken with the awareness he was not there. When I look at Alexius, I think how he will soon need a father, and his father is gone. It breaks my heart. When we eat the evening meal, Titus is not there to talk about things I never found interesting until I could no longer hear him. I miss him more than words can express."

"Sounds to me like you know now what true love is, and you are expressing your love for Titus very well."

"Livia, you sound wise yet I can't help but wonder, how would you know about love between a man and a woman?"

Livia answered, "What you don't know is I was married a long time ago. My husband was killed in an accident. I did love him a great deal. After he died, I lived with my father and Titus until he left for the army. I loved my father very much. When he died, I had no one to provide for me except Titus. I am so grateful that he has provided for me ever since father died."

"I never knew how you came to live with Titus. He never told me."

"He had no reason to tell you, nor did I until now. I just wanted you to know because I do know about love."

"Well, I confess, I did not know what genuine love was. But oh, I do know what it is now! This boat is not going fast enough to suit me. I don't know what it is like where we are going and I don't care. I just want to be with Titus."

"And so, you will be, but we cannot hurry this ship along. Try to concentrate on Alexius while we are at sea."

The days went by slowly and were marked by a hot sun and the nights that were cold, but each day Drusilla thought, "Another day closer."

IX

An Unbelievable Story

Titus was struggling as much as Drusilla. Both knew controlling time was impossible. It moved at its own speed and life continued in other ways. They were learning patience.

At a morning briefing Titus was only physically present, his mind focused on his family and where they might be at that moment. Emericus' voice brought Titus back to reality. "Cornelius, we still have an assignment we have not accomplished."

Titus refocused when he heard Emericus' voice. "We do?"

"Have you forgotten we are to investigate the situation in Capernaum? Is centurion Ludo maintaining Rome's welfare and is he fully functioning as a Roman officer? Do you remember that assignment?"

"Yes Sir. Tribune Arbelardus was very concerned about centurion Ludo's loyalty. Since we have a garrison there, Capernaum must be of some size and importance."

"Yes, it is not only a fishing city, it is important as a trade center as well. There are two major trade routes that go through the city. That means the city's influence goes to other places with the merchants that pass through. Roman presence is a must there. We must keep ourselves informed of the topics of conversation among the local people."

Titus said, "So, if a problem arose or talk of a rebellion started, it could spread to other areas quickly."

"You are right. It is time for us to investigate. I want you to go to Capernaum and see what the situation is there. All I have been able to find out about Ludo is he has an excellent relationship with the Jewish people. That is good unless it has clouded his mind. Even though there has not been any trouble in Capernaum, I have been told there is no fortification at all there, and that disturbs me. How can the army defend itself if the need to do so develops? I can only guess that Ludo believes that the Jews are completely trustworthy and will not attempt any revolt. He may have become too close to the Jews and could be fooled easily. Take only two men with you. I don't want to give Ludo the impression that his loyalty is in question. Be careful how you talk with him, and try not to make your visit appear to be an official investigation."

"If I can only take two men, I would like for Primus Constant to be one. I know that leaves no leadership for my centuria, but the decani are very capable. Primus is a good judge of men. That is why I would like for him to go."

"Very well, he may go, and pick one other man, but make him a legionary. I would like for you to leave in the morning."

"Yes, sir." Titus left and informed Primus they would be leaving in the morning. He told Primus to choose one man to go with them. Then he located Fishel. "I will pay you to guide me and two others to Capernaum. I need to leave in the morning. Can you go?"

"For you I will go. I will meet you at the east edge of the city at first light."

The next morning when they met, Titus instructed Fishel, "Take us the fastest way possible. I do not want to be gone any longer than necessary. My family should be on their way here, and I don't want to be gone when they arrive."

"I will do my best but it is normally a four day walk and the sun is hot. When it is not as hot, it can be done in 3 days if you walk longer every day." With that, they started. As they traveled, Titus explained to Primus and Fishel the reason for their trip. Then he swore them to secrecy.

By noon the next day, Titus thought they were traveling too slow and said so. Fishel said, "It is not wise to overwork yourself in this heat. We are on the most direct road to Capernaum. Be patient, my friend."

Each day Titus kept forcing himself to concentrate on his assignment. As they approached Capernaum, Titus asked Fishel, "Do you think the local people will answer me truthfully if I ask them questions?"

Fishel answered, "That depends on what you ask them. What is it you want to know?"

Titus continued, "I want to know something about their relationship with the centurion there, but I don't want them to know my motive for asking."

Fishel said,"If that is what you want to know, let me ask them. They will tell me more than they would tell you."

"I'm sure you are right. All right, see what you can find out; but this is just between you and me, understand?"

"I will tell only you what I learn."

Once they arrived in Capernaum, they went directly to Ludo's house. It was different than most of the other homes, which were small buildings. Ludo's house was not only larger, it was a two-story building, so it was easy to find. Ludo greeted them, "Welcome! Rest and refresh yourselves. We will have chai and food."

Since it was almost sundown, Ludo had his servants prepare a big meal for his guests. As they ate, Ludo asked, "What brings you to Capernaum with no legionaries?"

Titus had not thought about being asked that question. He blamed himself for not being better prepared. The question in his mind was," How do I answer without raising Ludo's suspicions?" He answered, "I am new to the area and have been asked to tour the cities and villages to see if any fortifications need to be repaired or improved."

Ludo was suspicious of the real reason for this visit but said nothing, instead he asked, "So, you are an engineer?"

"I have had some training in engineering." Titus answered, secretly hoping Ludo would not ask any questions about engineering. He realized the conversation was going in the wrong direction, and he needed to change the subject. Having previously mentioned the subject of fortifications, he said, "I noticed there are no fortifications at all here. I am very surprised."

"There is no need for any fortifications in Capernaum," Ludo replied. "The people here are very peaceable. They pay their taxes, and there has been no threat to me or to Rome."

Titus was surprised. He felt the local people were untrustworthy and this was a ridiculous answer so he said, "That may be true. However, if an outbreak should develop, how could you defend yourself without any fortification?"

Ludo felt the need to defend himself. He said, "I believe there will not be any outbreak in Capernaum because this city has been blessed by the God of the Jews. This city is special and I think it is because of one man who is special. He is the embodiment of peace. He is like no one you have ever met. He even has supernatural powers. He comes here from time to time but I never know when."

Titus asked, "Are you saying the peace here is because of one man?"

"Yes, it is true."

Titus was doubtful. He questioned the statement. "You can't expect me to believe one man can influence an entire city."

Ludo admitted, "You don't know the man. I know it sounds unbelievable, but it is true. I too was skeptical of him at first. I would like for you to meet him, but I have no idea where he is now."

Primus asked, "What is this man's name?"

Ludo replied, "The people here call him Jesus. Most say he is a prophet."

Titus was skeptical of all this and said, "I would like to meet such a man. When he comes back to Capernaum, will you send me word that he is here?"

"Yes, I will, but I have no thought of how long he might stay. He moves around a lot and does not stay in one place very long."

Titus asked, "You said he had supernatural power. Can you give me an example?"

Ludo took a deep breath and began, "I will tell you something you will have trouble believing. The servant that served us just now has been with me all of my adult life. I am very fond of him. Not long ago he became very sick. I thought he was going to die. I tried everything I knew. I even asked a local man who has knowledge of sicknesses to help. Nothing worked. I was willing to try anything. This man, Jesus was nearby, so I sent for him. With my own eyes I had seen this man cure people of blindness and of diseases. People walk all day just to hear him talk and be healed by him. I just knew he could help if he would. The only problem I saw was I am not a Jew, so I didn't know if he would help me or not. You see, a Jew cannot go into any building where a Roman lives or works. It has something to do with their religion.

"My messenger rushed back and told me that Jesus was on his way here. I did not want to cause a problem for him with his people by having him come inside my house. So, I sent a second messenger to tell him, he did not have to come into my house. He could just say the right words, and my servant would be healed. I truly believed that, and he must have believed me because he never came inside this house to see my servant. He just told my messenger that he was surprised I had that much faith in him, and because of my faith, my request would be granted. About the same time, my servant, fully healed, walked into the room where I was sitting, fully healed."

After listening, Titus commented, "Quite a story, but there has to be some reasonable explanation. Perhaps it was a coincidence."

"I said you would not believe it. I wouldn't either if it had not happened to me. All I can say is, what I have told you is true. Ask my servant if you wish. He will confirm what I just told you."

Primus asked, "How can a man have that kind of healing power?"

Ludo answered the question, "My only explanation is that he alludes to be the son of the Jewish God. The Jews believe in only one god. They call him, Yahweh."

Titus asked, "Does he say those words; I am the son of a god?" Ludo replied, "He does not say it outright, but you can hear it in his words. He says things like, "The Spirit of the Lord is on me." What he says leads one to believe nothing else. Maybe he is just a prophet; or maybe he is who he seems to be. I don't know, but how much different is that from a Caesar who says he is a god?"

Titus was quick to ask, "Are you criticizing Caesar?"

Ludo thought he might be in trouble, "No! no! I did not mean it that way. I just couldn't think of another example. I guess I am inclined to believe this man. His healing power is not natural but real. People seek him out for healing and to hear him speak. What he says to them has a calming effect on people. He is just so much different from everyone else that you want to listen to him."

Primus said, "You said he heals people. If he can heal people, he must be wealthy. How much does he charge for his healing?"

Feeling relieved, Ludo stated, "He does not charge anything."

"He is a Jew and does not charge? That is hard to believe."

"I said he was different."

Titus said, "If this man has that much power, what if he decided to incite the people to rebel against us? What would you do?"

"I would do my duty as a Roman centurion because I gave an oath to do so."

"Well said, Ludo."

Ludo responded, "I will add, I don't see this man as a trouble maker. I have heard him speak. He never says anything against Rome and he even says to pay taxes to Caesar. He seems to be more critical of the Jewish priests than Caesar. He encourages people to be good and to do good. He even says, 'Do not repay evil for evil.' He sets a high standard for people to follow."

Titus felt he had heard enough for now. "It has been a long day. If it is agreeable with you, I would like to retire for the night then talk some more in the morning."

"Certainly, I have no plans for tomorrow."

As Titus and Primus left, they both looked Ludo's servant over thoroughly but did not speak to him. When they were alone, Titus asked Primus, "What do you think about the story of healing Ludo's servant?"

Primus replied, "At the risk of saying Ludo is a liar, I find it very hard to believe."

"I agree, it is an unbelievable story. Let's see what else we discover. Tomorrow I'll talk to Ludo some more, and you talk to the legionaries and see if they are in fighting shape or if they have grown soft. You can tell me what you found on our return trip to Caesarea. I don't want anyone to overhear our conversations. We will leave the day after tomorrow."

The next day Titus and Ludo reviewed the legionaries in their morning parade. Afterward they walked through the city. As they walked and talked, Titus noticed the greetings from the local people toward Ludo were very warm. Their greetings were nothing like what he had experienced in Caesarea.

They stopped and Ludo said to Titus, "I know you came here to determine where my loyalty is and see if I was capable of remaining in charge of this centuria." Titus tried to interrupt, but Ludo held up his hand and said, "It's all right. Let me finish. I can guess my superior is concerned, but he need not be. I hope you will tell him that I am still loyal to Rome, Caesar, and the oath I took long ago. I will defend Rome against any enemies. However, I am a changed man. I look at things differently after living here."

Titus said, "I'm not sure what you mean by looking at things differently. Do you mean differently than when you first came to Judea? If that is what you mean, what has caused you to have this change?"

Ludo was hesitant in answering, "Yes, I think differently now from when I arrived. After listening to Jesus and seeing how the people changed because of what he had said or done. I am convinced he is not an ordinary man; he is special. He represents a change from everything I had ever known., but not in a bad way."

Titus was weighing everything he had seen and heard in his mind. He was anxious to hear what Primus and Fishel had to report. However, he would wait until they were on the return trip to Caesarea.

Ludo and Titus returned to Ludo's home and found Primus waiting for them. They told Ludo they would be leaving in the morning and Titus thanked Ludo for the tour of the city. He also reminded Ludo that he would like to know when Jesus returned to Capernaum.

Early the next morning they started the return trip to Caesarea. After walking for several hours, Titus called for an early stop as evening came. He wanted to compile all the information the three of them had learned. "Fishel, tell me what you found out."

Fishel began, "The people respect Ludo very much. He does not treat them as other Romans do. He has helped the poor and paid for their new synagogue. They say Ludo is just and fair in his dealings with them. They are hopeful that Ludo will stay. They told me that a man named Jesus influenced their thinking about Romans. They have no quarrel with you Romans, and they pay their taxes without complaining. I think this is due to Ludo. I have never seen a relationship between my people and you Romans like the one in Capernaum."

Titus thanked Fishel and asked, "What did you find out, Primus?"

"Ludo's legionaries are disciplined and in good shape. They are well-trained and would account for themselves in a battle. The legionaries also say the people are very peaceful and they don't anticipate any major trouble. They, too, have a high regard for Ludo. They say he believes there is only one God, the Jewish God, and they have no problem with his belief because of their respect for him. However, they do not believe in the Jewish God. They believe in the gods they learned about as children."

Titus made no comment, but he wrestled with the different influences he had found in Capernaum from other cities. All of these differences could be traced back to this man named Jesus. How could one man influence an entire city? How could a man, even a magician, heal a sick person without ever seeing him or not being with him? Did this really happen? If it did, there has to be some explanation for it.

On the second day they stopped at Nain for water. By talking with the people there, they learned that this Jesus had raised a widow's teenage son from the dead. Titus said to the man who told them this, "You can't mean what you are saying. No one can bring a dead person back to life."

The man replied, "It is true. I saw it with my own eyes. I was one of the mourners. It happened just as we went through the city gates to bury the widow's son. There were some people going into the city and a man in the group stopped us. Then he placed his hand on the dead man and told him to get up. We could not believe what was happening. We started to back away because he became unclean when he touched the dead body. To our amazement, the young man sat up and walked over to his mother. Ask some other people if you do not believe me."

Titus and Primus did ask some other people and heard a similar story. As they left, Titus said, "Were all these people drunk or what?"

Primus replied, "There has to be an explanation for whatever happened, or this man must have some kind of magical power from the gods. When people die, they are dead. People just don't come back to life. Do you think this could possibly be a rumor someone started?"

Fishel smiled and said, "If you were Jewish, you would understand that a prophet from Jehovah is among us."

"What are you talking about, Fishel? Explain it."

"Many years ago, we had a prophet named Isaiah who wrote that someday the Jews would have a new king who would be their savior. Isaiah prophesied we would know him by his ability to make blind people see, lame people walk, and to raise people from the dead. This man seems to be the one Isaiah wrote about."

Primus said, "Are you saying this man will be a king? Only Caesar will determine who is to be the king of this country. So, this man will not be king unless he plans to start a revolt. If that happens, the Roman army will stop him."

Titus entered the conversation, "The man that Ludo and the people in Capernaum have talked about did not sound like a revolutionist. But I agree with what you are saying Primus. We need to find out more about this man. Can you tell us more, Fishel?"

"I have told you all I know. I have never seen this man, but I have heard about him."

Titus asked, "Do you know where he can be found?"

"From what I have heard, he moves around a lot and does not have a permanent home."

Primus said, "That is what Ludo said too. How can he be found?"

There were no answers, just shrugs.

The rest of the way back to Caesarea, they talked about this man Jesus and the reasons why what they had been told could not be true. Just as they entered the city, Titus thanked Fishel and paid him for his help. He left the three Romans and seemed to vanish. Fishel did not want to be seen in public with a Roman centurion. Titus tried to respect Fishel's wishes.

Then they went directly to the fortress to report. Titus reported everything they had seen and been told. He even included the stories they heard in Nain.

Emericus listened intently, asking questions once in a while. Primus added several comments as well. After the two finished their report, Emericus said, "First, in your opinion, what should be done about Ludo?"

Titus was reluctant to say anything about a fellow centurion. His pause was obvious. Emericus encouraged him to speak. "I know what you are thinking. Be assured whatever you say will go no further and will not be used against either one of you. Whatever action is taken will come from me or higher up, not from you. Cornelius, I need you to tell me what you think. You were there and I was not. Therefore, you are in a better position to judge than I."

"Very well. Ludo said he is loyal to Rome and would remain so. I believe him. There are no problems with the people there. They pay their taxes and seem peaceful. In fact, they have an excellent relationship with Ludo which means a good relationship with Rome. Primus says the legionaries are fit and ready for any contingency. So my opinion is to leave Ludo in command. My only concern is there are no fortifications, but Ludo says they are not needed."

"Primus, do you agree with what Cornelius says?"

"I do. I was with Cornelius and saw and heard everything that he did, except when I was examining the legionaries."

"I accept your report. What I will advise is to leave Ludo in command in Capernaum. Now, who is this man Jesus you talked about? This is the first I have heard of him. Do you believe the stories you have heard about him?"

Titus answered, "All my experiences and everything I have been taught makes these stories unbelievable, but the people who told the stories sounded so convincing. Each time they would describe fully what they had experienced, without any hesitation. I just don't know if they were truthful or not. And I did see Ludo's servant who was said to be deathly ill, walking around in good health. I do not have an explanation for his recovery. So, I cannot say if what we were told is true or not true."

"I will write to Marcus and ask what he knows or has heard about this man. Tell your men to report anything they might hear as well. Until we know more, we will not waste our time on any investigations. You are dismissed."

"Yes, sir. Sir, have any ships arrived while we were gone?"

"No, but some local fishermen reported that there is a ship about a day out of port. It was somewhere north of here. If that is true, I would guess it will follow the coastline toward Caesarea when it gets within sight of land."

"Thank you for that information, sir." Both men left and headed to the bathhouse. They were ready to be refreshed.

"Titus, do you think your family is on that ship?"

"I don't know but I certainly hope so."

"I know you will be glad to reunite with them."

"Primus, I have missed them much more than I ever thought I would. My life is just not the same without them."

"I could tell that. You have been more on edge since we have been here."

"I didn't know it was that obvious. I am sorry if I have been difficult to work with."

As they left the bathhouse, Primus said, "I think I could sleep for two days." Titus was not sure he could sleep at all. He was anxious for the next day to begin.

He didn't sleep. He laid in bed reprocessing everything he had heard Ludo say and what he learned in Nain. Recalling the conversation with Primus on the way to Judea, Titus wondered if a great power did exist. No answer came to him. Later, his mind shifted to thoughts of his family arriving. He hoped it would be before the next day ended.

X

A Second Beginning

As the first rays of the sun broke over the horizon, Titus was up and dressed for the day. He started toward the dock when he saw a young boy sitting beside the road. He told the boy he would pay him to go to the dock and watch for a ship. As soon as he saw one, he was to run to the fortress and tell him.

After the boy agreed, Titus went to perform his daily duties. He was so anxious that he had trouble concentrating on his duties. The day passed and the sun was touching the horizon, there had been no word from the boy. Titus walked down to the dock and found the boy still there. He gave him a coin and said, "If you come back tomorrow and do the same thing, I will give you another coin." Then Titus walked slowly to the place his family would call home for the next few years. Disappointment could be seen on his face. The ship, if there was one, was more than a day away.

Had Emericus been misinformed? Had the ship developed a problem? Was the ship in some danger? Many questions kept going through Titus' mind.

The night was long, and Titus couldn't sleep. Finally, he gave up trying and sat outside, looking at the moon. He wondered if Drusilla was looking at the moon at the same time. He said aloud, "Since we have been separated, I realize how much I have missed you, Drusilla. I keep seeing you in my mind. I just want to lie with you and hold you close. I want to be with Alexius. I wonder how much he has grown. Where is that ship?" There was no one to hear his words. The morning could not come soon enough.

The next morning, he left early for the fortress, wanting to keep busy doing something. It did not matter what he did, anything that occupied his mind would do. Later, when Primus reported, Titus told him, "I expect the ship carrying my family will arrive today. When it does, I will leave to greet them and escort them to our home. Please take charge of things for me."

Primus replied, "There is very little going on right now. If something happens that needs attention, I'll take care of it."

Every so often Titus would walk outside and look to see if the boy was coming. Around the middle of the day, he saw the boy running toward him. The expression on Titus' face changed in an instant and he ran to meet the boy.

"There is a ship coming into the dock!" He gave the boy two coins and hurried to the dock. By the time he got there the ship had come along side of the dock. Men were securing the ship with ropes and the gangplank was connecting it to the dock. His eyes searched the ship's railing and they were rewarded. Drusilla and Livia were waving to him. He waved back with a big smile on his face. The two women came down the gangplank, and a little boy was trying to walk with them, but his mother picked him up in order to move faster. Titus' smile could not have been wider. His family had arrived.

Drusilla threw her arms around his neck and kissed him. Livia hugged him as best she could with Drusilla still locked onto him and Alexius somewhere between them. Although public displaying of affection was considered unbecoming to a centurion, Titus didn't care who saw them or what they might think. Protocol just did not matter. He was overjoyed at seeing his family. The little boy watching and hearing his mother cry was wondering who this man was and why his mother was crying.

When the three broke apart, Titus reached out and took Alexius into his arms. Alexius started to cry and reached for his mother. Titus was surprised and his face showed it. He handed the boy back to Drusilla. He was disappointed at the boy's reaction. She said, "It's all right, Alexius, this is your father." Turning to Titus, Drusilla reassured him, "Do not be concerned. He does not know you. A child's reaction to an unknown person is to cry. He will be fine after the two of you get reacquainted."

As Titus and his family stood talking, Coto came down the gangplank loaded down with baskets and boxes. Titus said, "Coto, good to see you. Just wait and I will get someone to help you."

"Thank you, I would appreciate help because there is more." Titus laughed, "I could have guessed". The reunited family took their first steps toward their new home. The ladies stumbled. Titus grabbing both of them, said, "It will take a day or two for your feet to realize you are on solid ground."

At end of the dock were some young men. Titus approached one and pointed as he said, "I will pay you to help that man back there carry things to our house." The young man agreed and Titus told him where to go. While Titus was talking with the young man, Drusilla and Livia marveled at the sight in front of them. Straight out from the end of the dock there were steps leading up to a temple on a high hill. Livia said, "What an impressive temple."

Titus told them "Yes, it is. All gods can be worshipped there."

As the family walked through the city, Titus started telling them about the land and the people. "The city's population is about 65% Jews, and the rest are a mixture of Greek, Syrian, and Arabian people."

As they walked, Drusilla and Livia begin to notice they were drawing stares from curious onlookers. The few European women who lived in Caesarea were rarely seen in public. Even though Caesarea was a mixture of different cultures and was tolerant of different religions, these two women stood out because their heads were not covered. Fortunately, there were no problems, but such scrutiny made the two women feel uncomfortable. Livia asked, "Titus why is everyone staring at us?"

Being a male, Titus had not noticed this before. He said, "It must be because your hair is not covered and your clothes are different which marks you as a foreigner. This does not mean anything unsafe. It is just unusual to them."

After arriving at their new home, the women examined every room, then registered their approval. Seeing that his family was settled in their new home, Titus returned to the fortress. First, he sought Emericus. Finding him in his quarters, Titus stated his request, "Sir, my family has just arrived. I request to be relieved of my duties for three or four days so that I might spend some time with them."

"Your centuria is not scheduled for a patrol for the next two weeks so, I think the army could get along without you for three or four days. Go and join your family then report back in four days."

Titus was overjoyed when Emericus granted his request. Then he searched for Primus. He informed Primus, "I will be at home for the next four days. I know you can take care of everything, but, if you do need me, send someone for me."

Primus said, "Your family must have arrived."

"Yes, they did. I plan to spend the next four days with them."

"Go! Enjoy yourself. I will take care of everything here."

Titus got home late that afternoon. He was so elated he did not know what to do or say first. Drusilla resolved that by kissing him and saying, "It is wonderful that we are together again."

He spent what was left of the day with Alexius and the two slowly began to bond. Livia prepared a meal from what food she could find, which allowed Drusilla to be with Titus. It was difficult for her because Titus had not purchased any seasonings or any of the same food she would have bought. She felt she had been successful when Titus announced, 'That was the best meal I had had in months."

Later Titus asked Coto if there were any problems on their voyage. He was relieved when Coto said there were no problems.

When it was time to retire for the night, Drusilla put her arms around Titus and said, "I did not think our separation would ever end. I missed you so much. Each night I would lie alone in bed wondering where you were and what you had done that day. Our time apart made me realize how much I love you. I thought I knew what it meant to love someone before we were married. But I was wrong. Our being apart these last few months have given me a deeper understanding of love."

Titus held Drusilla's hand and kissed her, "I feel the same. I am so glad you are here. Drusilla, I need to make a confession. When I first thought about marriage, I was mostly interested in having a son, a legitimate heir. I liked you and thought of you as a good woman capable of bearing and raising my son. However, our time apart has made me realize how much I love you, how much I want to be with you, and how much you mean to me. I love you, Drusilla."

"I'm glad you told me, Titus, and I need to confess as well. Before you asked my father about marrying me, he was continually berating me for refusing to marry the man he had chosen for me. He would often predict that I would go to my grave a lonely dried up old woman. You provided a way of escape from his constant chastisement. I saw in you an opportunity for security and social position. In the few years we have been married I have grown to love you and our son more than I have ever loved anyone or anything in my life. Now, you are my life."

Titus smiled and kissed her again. "We both have changed and I am glad. Let's start all over again. To start tell me everything you have been doing. I want to hear what has been keeping you occupied."

"No, you don't; you would soon be bored. You tell me what you have been doing."

"We'll talk tomorrow." There was no more conversation, but very little sleep that night.

The next day he introduced Drusilla and Livia to Caesarea. He showed them the fortress, the marketplace, the temple, and different areas of the city. When they returned to their new home, Titus' arms were full of food the ladies had purchased. The four days that followed were full of joy. Titus played with Alexius and listened to stories of everything that he was learning to do and things he had said.

The nights were warm and tender with two people united in blissful love. Titus had never been so happy and contented. He did not want this time to go by so fast. In fact, he hoped it would never end.

When it was close to the time for Titus to resume his duties, he cautioned the two women, "It would be wise for Coto to escort you whenever you walked through the city. You will be safe when you go out; but in this culture, it is best for you to be with a man." He also told the women to keep their heads covered when they were in public. This would make them blend in better with the local women.

Titus' four-day leave ended. He returned to his daily duties at the fortress a very contented man. His daily routine changed. Now at the end of the day, whenever it was possible, he would return to his home to spend the evening with his family. After playing with Alexius, he and Drusilla would share the details of their day, growing deeper in their love for each other.

Primus was given most of the patrols that required being gone more than one day. Titus was very content with the way life was going, but Primus did not share his opinion. He was growing weary of having so many overnight patrols passed on to him, and he hoped this would not be a permanent arrangement.

Living in a different land and culture was an adjustment for Drusilla and Livia. They had much to learn. Language was sometimes a barrier. They had no knowledge of the Jewish language. However, their knowledge of Greek helped since the Greek language was more prevalent in this part of the world than the Roman language.

The second adjustment was adapting to the different culture. Shopping for food was the first thing they noticed. Some foods were much better such as the fresh fruit, but some foods they were accustomed to buying were hard to find. Then they discovered Jewish shops were not open on Saturdays. When they did go to a Jewish shop, the shopkeepers were suspicious of them. Drusilla and Livia soon learned that if they sent Coto to buy food and necessities, they would avoid the suspicious looks. That was not a problem if Titus was with them. The people either respected or feared a centurion. Drusilla was not sure which.

When fall arrived, Pontius Pilate sent word to Caesarea that he was coming to tour the area. In honor of the occasion, there was to be a performance by some well-known Greek actors. Plans were made for a celebratory event which would require additional military presence at the theater. Titus' centuria was selected for that duty. Drusilla and Livia wanted to attend, and Titus saw no problem with their going. He had to be there anyway so why not let his wife and sister be there as well.

After the plans were made for Pilate's security, Titus said to Primus, "I am going to sit with my wife and sister during the performance. Why don't you plan to sit with us? There is no need for you to be standing in some aisle."

"Thank you. It does sound better than standing half the night."

During the performance, Primus sat next to Livia. He had met her when he was reunited with Titus and had seen her a few times after that, but he had never paid much attention to her. To him, Livia was Titus' older sister and two or three years older than he. After sitting beside her for over an hour, he began to notice her more than the performance. Livia became aware that Primus was watching her but said nothing. Although the two did engage in some trivial conversation, nothing meaningful was said.

As the performance came to an end, Titus told the women to stay seated, that he and Primus had to see to Pilate's departure. They would be back as soon as Pilate was gone. Pilate, however, wanted an armed escort to his lodging for the night. Titus said to Primus, "Since you have taken most of the patrols lately, I'll escort Pilate and you escort the ladies home." Primus was more than happy to do so. He did so shyly and said very little.

Over the next few weeks, Primus found excuses to go to Titus' home. It took a while, but Titus finally realized Primus' excuses for his visits were centered in his growing interest in Livia. He said, "Primus, as long as Livia wants your company, you are welcome. You don't need an excuse to see her. Come, whenever you want."

Primus replied, "I didn't know how to ask you because of our friendship and the difference in rank. It made asking awkward."

"We have known each other for a long time; the difference in rank is not important when we are not on duty. It never has been. I thought you knew that."

"Well, I guess I should tell you the real reason. I was hesitant because you know all my faults, and I was afraid you might think I was not good enough for your sister."

"I know all your good points, too. I do not and will never think you are not good enough for Livia. She will decide that on her own."

After Livia and Primus had been seeing each other for a month, Drusilla said to Titus, "I think you are going to have a brother-in-law very soon."

"I'm not surprised. I have noticed changes in Primus."

One evening sometime later, a messenger arrived at Titus' home with a message from Ludo.

The messenger announced, "Sir, Centurion Ludo sends you greetings and asks that you to come quickly because Jesus has returned to Capernaum."

Titus sent the messenger back to Ludo instructing him to keep Jesus in Capernaum until he could get there.

As soon as the messenger left, Drusilla, who overheard the conversation between Titus and the messenger, asked, "Who is this man that seems to be so important to you?"

Titus answered, "This man is said to have miraculous healing powers. He is developing a growing following. Ludo thinks he is from the gods. Well really just one god. If this man is that powerful, he could develop a rebellious following and become dangerous. I need to make sure he is not planning to lead a revolution against Rome."

"Does that mean you must go? I feel so lost when you are not here at night. I think now is as good a time as any to tell you that we are going to have another baby."

"Really? When?"

"I think in five months or a little longer."

"Now I understand why you don't want me gone for a long period of time. Your news has changed my plans. I will send Primus to Capernaum and have him bring this Jesus here. I must go to the fortress and talk to Primus now. This man might not stay in Capernaum very long."

Drusilla was so pleased. "Thank you for staying, Titus!"

Titus found Primus at the barracks where he thought Primus would be. He said, "Primus, Drusilla is going to have a baby and has asked me to stay nearby. Yet Ludo has sent word that Jesus is in Capernaum. Would you go there in my place and bring Jesus back here?"

Primus grinned and said, "So you are going to be a father again! Well, for Drusilla's sake, I'll go."

"Funny! Thank you. Go and take two contubernia with you and ask Ludo where you can find Jesus. Then bring him back here for questioning. Arrest him if you have to."

"I will leave immediately."

Eight days later, Primus returned but without Jesus. He told Titus, "Jesus left Capernaum before I arrived. Ludo explained he had no reason to arrest or hold Jesus.

"No one seemed to know where Jesus went. One person told me of a village where he thought Jesus was going. So, I went to that village and one other, looking for Jesus, but the man seemed to just disappear. The people in the villages told me he does not stay in one place very long."

"We missed our chance, but I am sure you did all you could."

"Titus, while I was there, I was told another unbelievable story about this man that I verified was true."

"What did this Jesus do now?"

"Remember when we went through Nain and heard the story about this Jesus bringing a widow's son back to life?"

"Yes, I remember that but did not believe it. It is impossible to bring someone back from the dead."

"I don't disagree, but he did it again"

"What? I don't believe it. Tell me what you heard."

"The head priest in Capernaum had a 12-year-old daughter who died. Six different people verified she was dead. At the priest's request, Jesus went to his house and went inside. No one saw what he did or said, but shortly thereafter, the girl walked outside, thanking Jesus and telling him goodbye. These six people swear they saw her dead before his visit. After his visit she was alive. I quizzed three of the six people, and their stories were identical. Then I talked to the girl. She said all she remembers is being sick and falling asleep, then waking up and feeling better than she had felt in weeks. She said she remembers seeing her mother crying and a strange man talking to her."

Titus asked, "Do you think this is a true account?"

"It's hard for me to think otherwise. There is more. I was told that while this Jesus was going to the priest's house, he stopped and healed some woman who had a serious bleeding problem."

"Who is this man? What you are telling me is not humanly possible. Yet, it is happening. Is some god involved? If Jesus is a god, does he have something in mind besides healing people? I always thought the gods did not mix with people. Am I wrong? Could a god be physically among people?

"If he is not one of the gods, then where does he get this magical power to heal and even bring dead people back to life? I have never been more perplexed."

"I don't understand how these things could happen either, Titus. I am just telling you what I learned." The day ended with both men very perplexed.

After their evening meal Titus shared with Drusilla all he knew about Jesus and of the miracles he had performed.

She said, "All this sounds like a story you might tell a child. Do you really think it is true?"

"I am not sure what to believe and what not to believe. I know what I heard from some people was very convincing. This new story that Primus told me makes me wonder. Everything he told me goes against everything I have ever been taught or discovered in life. However, it is difficult for me to say it is not true. I feel Primus is convinced the stories are true, but logic tells me they cannot be true. I don't know what to think. I have to find out more about this man. I must find out who is he."

"Do you think he is a threat to peace here?"

"I don't think so, but I am not certain. That is why I need to know more. I am going to talk to Emericus in the morning and see if he wants to take any action."

That night, Titus lay with his arms around Drusilla. He could feel her enlarged stomach. His mind was briefly distracted from Jesus. He asked, "Do you think it will be a boy or a girl?"

"I don't know. You will have to wait and see."

XI

The Day the Earth Shook

In the morning when the sun reached the mid-point, Titus located Primus and asked him to tell Emericus firsthand about the daughter of the priest in Capernaum and the new information he had obtained about the man called Jesus. The two of them found Emericus still in his quarters. After Primus had given his report to Emericus, Titus added, "Sir, this man seems to have power we do not understand."

Emericus asked, "Do you feel this man is a threat?"

"I really don't know. Centurion Ludo believes he is a peaceable man. My concern is if he is as powerful as the reports make him out to be, and he decided to influence his followers to oppose Rome, we could be facing a very dangerous situation."

"Is there any evidence that he has gathered men or weapons?"

Titus replied, "No. From what I hear, he has a lot of followers, but they are both men and women and many of them are seeking healing. Everything seems to be peaceable."

Primus intervened, 'Titus, when Emericus asked if Jesus had gathered men, I remember one more thing I didn't tell you."

"What was that?"

"I'm not sure I would say he gathered men but I learned that one time there were 5000 or more men that followed him out into some desolate area about 20 stadia east of Capernaum. But they were not a rebellious group because there were women and children with them."

"Do you know the purpose of this gathering or how long it went on?" asked Emericus.

"From what I heard these people went just to hear him talk and to be healed of afflictions. One man that went, told me it was a great talk that made him feel at peace and wanting to know more about their God. There was nothing said about anyone having weapons. As for how long it went on, they were there most of the day."

Titus asked, "Did you hear about any advanced preparations for this gathering?"

"No, it just seemed to happen. There were no supply packs or water jars. No evidence of any kind of support."

Emericus asked, "If they had no supplies, how did they feed them?"

Primus answered, "Apparently someone in the crowd had some food and it was shared by everyone and there was left over food for people to take with them."

Titus was amazed, "How could one person have enough food with him to feed that many people?"

"I don't know, Titus. It baffles me too."

After thinking about what he had heard, Emericus said, "That is quite an account, but it doesn't sound threatening. I believe we should wait a while and see what happens. It was not that long ago that there was the threat of a revolt in Jerusalem because of the emperor's attempt to place a statue of himself in the Jewish temple. I don't want to give these people any excuse to start talking of a revolt again. In the meantime, keep your eyes and ears open to any new reports about this man and keep me informed of his movements."

"Yes sir. We will try, but this man does not stay in one place very long. It is difficult to keep up with his location."

Emericus was not satisfied with Titus' answer. He wanted another source of information. He told Titus and Primus, "I will ask Marcus what he has heard or knows about this Jesus."

A messenger was sent to Jerusalem with questions about Jesus. Marcus reported back to Emericus, that he knew about Jesus because of all the talk among the local people about him and his healing powers. But he had heard nothing connecting Jesus to any unrest or uprising.

No more reports of Jesus were heard in Caesarea for several days.

A month went by, then two months, daily chores and routines were the norm for Titus and his family. Then reports began to trickle in about miracles Jesus had performed in different towns, but there was never any indication of a revolt.

Each time the reports related miraculous stories of astonishing events that surrounded Jesus. Titus' curiosity about this man grew and more unanswered questions filled his mind. He asked Primus, "Who is this man? How can we find him?"

"I don't know, Titus. He does not appear to be a normal man. I wonder about him myself."

The more Titus heard, the more obsessed he became with this man called Jesus. Thoughts about him totally preoccupied his mind. He was determined to find and question him. He planned to leave the next day and start his search for him in Capernaum. The only reservation he had was how to tell Drusilla because of her request for him to stay near her.

Later that afternoon at the Tribune's monthly officers' meeting, a messenger from Jerusalem walked into the room seeking Emericus. The messenger began talking to Emericus very softly, trying not to interrupt the meeting. But Titus, sitting next to Emericus could hear what was said, and he was shocked when he heard that Pilate had ordered Jesus' crucifixion. It had been carried out immediately. Marcus thought Emericus should know what happened since he had asked about Jesus. But he had waited a day to make sure there wasn't any threat of an uprising. before he had sent the messenger to Caesarea with the report.

Emericus asked aloud, "How long ago did the execution occur?" Most in the room heard the question and all other conversation stopped. "Five days ago." was the reply.

All the officers' attention focused on Emericus' conversation with the messenger, when they heard him ask, "Was there any disturbance or fighting?" There was no other conversation in the room. It was very quiet.

"None whatsoever! In fact, the Jewish religious leaders were almost in a celebratory mood." said the messenger.

Emericus, realizing that all the officers were listening, told the messenger to tell aloud all he knew about Jesus' crucifixion. He knew everyone needed to know what was happening. Just about all of them had heard about Jesus, but the news of his death did not affect them like it did Titus.

Upon completion of the messenger's story of Jesus' crucifixion, Emericus followed up with him "So the execution was calm and without incident?"

"Not exactly, sir. Following the execution some very unusual things happened."

"What sort of unusual things happened?" one of the officers asked.

The messenger was beginning to feel uncomfortable in front of all the officers. He looked around the room biting his lower lip. Emericus reassured him saying, "You are doing a fine job of telling us what happened, continue. You are free to say whatever you want."

The messenger said, "Well, for one thing, in the middle of the day the sun just disappeared; it was as dark as night for three hours. Life in the city came to a complete stand still as people came out of their homes and shops. They were standing in the streets asking one another what was going on when suddenly there was an earthquake. The whole world just shook and shook. People could be heard screaming all over the city. People were afraid.

"Another thing that bothered me was the way Marcus looked when he returned from the execution. His face was white and he seemed confused. Always before he had been rock-solid, nothing seemed to upset him. This time he stuttered and stammered as he ordered every available man to be armed and ready for battle. The entire centuria did not know what to expect."

Emericus said, "Earthquakes are not too unusual in this part of the country, and this darkness, could it have been caused by an incoming storm?"

"No sir. The darkness spread over the land too quickly and it was darker than a starless night at midnight. It was more like the gods were angry with us and they covered up the sun."

"Are you telling us that this sudden darkness and severe earthquake may have been caused by the gods?" asked Emericus.

"I don't know, sir," said the messenger. "I don't think anyone knows the cause."

The tribune who had been listening to all that was said, asked the messenger, "Is your report what Marcus told you to say, or are the words your choice?"

Nervously the messenger answered, "My words, sir. It was a day that I never want to experience again."

Emericus wanted to be certain nothing was missing in the messenger's report but first he tried to make the messenger feel at ease. He said, "Sounds like the day was very different than any other day." And then he asked, "Was there anything else you could tell us from what you experienced?"

"No sir, but there were a few odd reports of strange things happening that day, such as people reporting they saw people who had been dead, walking around the city."

An officer across the room said, "That is hard to believe; dead people don't walk."

The messenger told him, "I know, sir. But after being there myself, I would believe anything anyone told me!"

One of the officers asked, "Did anyone have any explanations for what happened?"

"No, sir."

Emericus asked, "As for the earthquake, did it do much damage?"

The messenger, with a smile on his face, said, "There were some buildings and a few homes damaged but no reports of death. One thing that was humorous, the Jewish priests were all upset because some curtain in their temple was torn. With all that occurred that day, can you imagine getting upset because a curtain was damaged? "

Emericus brought the interview to a close by saying, "Thank you for bringing us this information. You may return to Jerusalem."

By now the original purpose of the meeting was lost. Many conversations began among officers giving opinions on whether the gods caused these events. Titus just quietly left the meeting, regretting the death of Jesus. He felt cheated because now he would never find out Jesus's true identity or if he truly had special powers or not. He was devasted by the news of Jesus' death. The other news of unusual happenings was of no interest to him.

Once home, he told Drusilla and Livia that Jesus had been executed. Drusilla asked, "What criminal thing did Jesus do that warranted his execution?"

"I'm not sure what he did, if anything. The messenger never said anything about that."

Coto, who had overheard the conversation, asked, "How was he executed?"

Titus answered, "He was crucified on a cross. It is a horrible way to die."

Drusilla put her hand on Titus's arm and said, "Titus, you have been obsessed with finding this man. That was all you seemed to have on your mind the last few days. Now he is dead. So, forget about him. You have a family to consider. Think about having a new baby in the house."

"I suppose you are right."

Life returned to normal for the next few days. Then Drusilla went into labor and delivered a baby girl. She wanted to name her Adela, after her grandmother. Titus was so thrilled that Drusilla was well, he didn't care what name was chosen. His feelings toward his wife were totally different than when Alexius was born. This time he went to Drusilla without being prompted by Livia.

Afterward he asked Alexius what he thought about having a baby sister. Alexius said, "Why didn't you get a boy? What can you do with a girl?" Titus just laughed, and Alexius stomped out of the room.

While Drusilla was recovering, Titus tried to be at home as much as possible during the day, but he had military obligations at the fortress that were mandatory and required his time. Drusilla felt there were too many hours he was required to be gone. Plus, sleepless nights caring for the new baby added to the strain of his absence. Titus was grateful that Livia was supportive and helpful.

Adela was barely a month old when Titus received instructions to report to Emericus. Who was very concerned because another messenger had arrived from Jerusalem? Marcus' optio had sent him. Emericus said to Titus, as he handed the message to him, "I don't know if this has any connection to the message we received not that long ago about the crucifixion of Jesus or not. Tell me what you make of it."

The message read, Sir, you had better come to Jerusalem. Something is wrong with Centurion Marcus. He just sits and stares at the sky and keeps saying, "I did it." After reading it, Titus said, "I don't understand it at all."

Emericus asked the messenger, "Is he doing any of his duties?"

"No sir, he just sits and stares. The men are wondering what is going on and what they should do."

Without any hesitation Emericus instructed Titus, "Centurion Cornelius, you go back with this messenger and find out what is going on. Maybe Marcus needs some kind of medical help. If so, get him whatever he needs. If he is not functioning properly, then you stay and send word back to me. If a replacement is needed, I will send one as soon as possible."

Titus replied, "Yes, sir."

"And Cornelius, you should leave today. I don't want to see a void in leadership in Jerusalem. Conditions there could become volatile if the Jews find out about Marcus and believe the army is leaderless."

Titus rushed home to explain that he would be gone for a few days. He said to Drusilla, "I have been ordered to go to Jerusalem because the centurion there is sick. I don't know how long I will be gone; I could be gone for a while, but I will return as quickly as possible." He knew Drusilla would be unhappy; however, he did not have any choice in the matter. No matter what he said, he was not successful in helping her understand. Drusilla could not grasp why her husband was being ordered to go to Jerusalem just because someone was sick.

He left for Jerusalem with the messenger an hour later. His heart was very heavy. He felt trapped between being given an order to leave immediately and his inability to help Drusilla understand why he had left.

Three days later he arrived in Jerusalem. He went directly to Marcus' quarters. Just as the messenger had said, he found Marcus sitting, rocking back and forth, saying, "I did it. I am doomed!" He had lost weight. His eyes were sunken back into his face and he was only half dressed. His servant told Titus that Marcus rarely ate or drank.

"How long has he been like this?" asked Titus.

"For more than ten days. I don't remember when it first started," came the reply.

Titus sat down facing Marcus. "Marcus, do you know who I am?"

Marcus stopped for a minute and said, "Of course, you are Cornelius." Then he went back to rocking and saying, "I did it."

"What did you do, Marcus?"

"I killed God's son. I am doomed."

"What are you talking about? You didn't kill a son of one of the gods."

"Yes, I did. He was not a son of one of the gods. He was the Son of The God, the one the Jews worship."

"All right, tell me about it."

Marcus stopped rocking and looked at Titus. Then he began, "The Jewish priests had captured Jesus, and they took him to Pilate. They wanted him killed. That was very obvious. They accused him of one thing but then brought a different accusation when they saw Pilate doubted their accusations or found them trivial. He thought the entire issue had to do with their religion and told the Jews they should settle the problem themselves. But the Jews replied, 'No! No! The man should die, and by Roman law we cannot execute him.'

"Finally, the priests told Pilate that Jesus claimed to be king of the Jews. That got Pilate's attention. He questioned Jesus, 'Did you say you were king of the Jews?'

Jesus told Pilate, 'Yes, but my kingdom is not of this world.' That did not make any sense to Pilate. More questioning revealed that he was from Galilee. When Pilate heard that, he thought he could escape involvement in the case. So he told me to take him to King Herod. Pilate thought that would end his part in the matter. It didn't. Herod told me to take him back to Pilate."

Titus was very attentive to what Marcus was telling him. "What happened then?"

Marcus continued, "The Jews came back demanding an execution. Pilate didn't think the man was guilty of anything deserving death, and he told the Jews that. They just kept on accusing the man. Pilate then ordered me to take him out and whip him. I know he thought when the Jews saw blood, they will be satisfied.

"So, I did. The man never let out one cry the entire time he was being whipped. I ordered my men to whip him harder and still he was silent. I had never seen such a reaction. When I took him back covered in blood, I was surprised he could even stand after the beating we gave him. Most men would have passed out. When the Jews saw him standing there, blood dripping, they had no pity. They still yelled, 'Crucify him!'

"I don't think Pilate ever thought Jesus deserved to die, so he made one more attempt to end things without killing him. He gave them a choice of releasing Jesus or a criminal named Barabbas. They chose Barabbas! Pilate gave up and told me to take Jesus out and crucify him. So I did. There were two others I was to crucify, so one more did not matter to me."

Marcus paused and whimpered a little, then he continued, "I sent two men out to dig the holes and get the logs for posts. While they were doing that, the rest of the men wanted to have some fun with the guy. It was all right with me. I was in a bad mood anyway because Pilate had ordered me to take charge of him. The assignment could have been handled by a decanus. It was not worthy of my time, so I didn't mind at all. I thought he was just some crazy Jew.

"They roughed him up more than they usually did criminals, but he did not say anything. They made fun of him and hit him over and over again. I thought it was strange that he didn't at least cry out in pain. Most of the time a person pleads for mercy, but not Jesus. It was as if he had supernatural strength. Then the men started mocking him about being a king. I sat there watching and laughing with my men.

"When we got tired of that, we started toward the crucifixion site. The men gave Jesus a cross to carry to the crucifixion site. He was so weak he fell twice. The second time, I heard a commotion behind me. I turned around and saw he was on the ground and people were trying to give him water. I began to believe Jesus might not make it to the crucifixion site. So I told one of my men to get a bystander to carry his cross. I hoped he could walk the rest of the way on his own. He got up, and we started forward.

"After we got to the crucifixion site, I discovered we didn't bring enough rope for all three crucifixions, so we nailed Jesus to the cross. He still said nothing while we were doing it. We raised up the cross and worked it toward the hole and dropped it in. Then we sat down and waited for the three guys to die. But this time it was different."

Titus asked Marcus," What do you mean, different?"

Marcus answered, "The Jewish priests were there and they began shouting, 'if you are the son of Yahweh then come down off that cross!"

"I'll agree it is unusual for priests to be at a crucifixion. Who is Yahweh?" Titus had forgotten Ludo had used the word, Yahweh.

"That is the name of their God. Cornelius, before Jesus died other things happened that were not normal."

Suddenly all the things Ludo had told him surfaced in Titus' memory. He began remembering the other stories about Jesus doing miracles and now he hears the words, not normal. He wanted to know more so he asked, "Like what?"

Marcus began, "About the sixth hour, the sun disappeared for three hours. It got so black you could not see your hand in front of your face, and the wind blew so strong people could not stand up. I didn't try to stand. I was still setting on the ground when daylight began to return. Suddenly I noticed Jesus looking at me, - straight at me! His eyes were like no one's eyes I had ever seen. I don't know how to describe his eyes except there was no hatred in them, instead they were full of compassion. I had never had this kind of experience before. It was the first time in my life that I was actually afraid.

"I heard him say, 'Father forgive them.' I was killing him, but he was asking his father to forgive me. How can a man talk about forgiveness when you are killing him? I just could not understand that. It was then that I knew this was not an ordinary man. A lightning bolt struck the ground right behind me. I fell on my face. I thought I would pass out. Suddenly I knew, I was killing the Son of God! My guts churned as if a knife was stuck in my stomach. Even now, I can still see his eyes looking at me."

"Marcus stop! I don't know who this man was, but, you did not order him to be killed. Pilate did. You were just following orders."

"No, I treated him terribly and killed him."

"Even if you did, what makes you think he was the son of God?"

"The darkness, the roaring wind, and did I tell you there was an earthquake? I did, didn't I? Well, the earth shook like I have never experienced before. People tried to run, but they just fell down. There were so many things that happened that can't be explained. And the way he died! I have never seen anyone die the way Jesus died. It was almost as if he was in control of what was happening. He would determine when he would be dead. After he was dead, I almost ran back to the fortress. I thought it was all over and I wanted to forget the entire mess. It wasn't over."

Titus had been listening intently. He expected Marcus to end his story but was surprised at Marcus' last comment. He asked, "What do you mean It wasn't over?"

Marcus said, "There are some more things which you are not going to believe."

"Let me be the judge of that. What else can you tell me?"

"After Jesus was buried, Pilate ordered us to guard his tomb for three days. I set up a three-man guard detail to be changed on a 12-hour rotation. The first exchange was to occur shortly after day break. When the second guard detail arrived at the tomb, the first three men were not there and the tomb had been opened. It was empty. There was no body inside. There was uneaten food, the men's spears and blankets were there but no Legionaries either alive or dead. They were men with good records. The three have never reported back nor have they been located. I had patrols out looking for them but they have not found a trace of the deserters. Something out of the ordinary had to have happened that caused them to disappear. They know what happened. But I'll never know unless I can question them.

"Then I talked to some Jews a week ago, and they told me they had seen Jesus and heard him speak. This is when I knew I was doomed. He was not dead. Dead people do not talk, and I know he was dead. I saw him die. One of my men put a spear in his side. Immediately blood and water flowed out. He was dead! Now he is alive! I know it, and he is going to take his revenge on me."

"Marcus, I cannot explain what has happened, but you must get hold of yourself and resume your duties as a centurion. You cannot let this man's death consume you. You are responsible for the peace in this city. Your men expect you to lead them."

"I cannot lead anybody. It is too late for me to do anything. I am just waiting to be struck down. I hope it is by the sword and not by fire. Cornelius, I don't care what happens to this city. I don't care what happens to Rome. I don't care about anything. You do whatever you have to do. I am just waiting to be killed. I am doomed!"

"Very well. You leave me no choice but to recommend a replacement for you. You were a good centurion, Marcus."

Titus left Marcus and called the legionaries together and announced he would assume command. Next, he sent a report by messenger to Emericus that Marcus should be relieved of his command and replaced. "Tell him I will assume Marcus's duties until a replacement arrives", he instructed the messenger. The following day Titus had two contubernia escort Marcus to Caesarea.

Titus' obsession with Jesus began all over again. His mind focused on the question of Jesus' identity. Titus remembered Marcus had said some people had seen Jesus alive. "Will I ever find out about him? Is it possible that Jesus is alive?" From then on Titus' days were consumed with thoughts about Jesus. He asked everyone with whom he came into contact if they knew anything about Jesus. He had men searching for people who might have had contact with Jesus so he could question them.

No one was found who would admit they knew Jesus.

Then one day a report came in about a dead body on the edge of town. Titus took some men and went to investigate. The body was bruised and bloody and surrounded with rocks. Titus asked some bystanders, "What happened here?" No one said a word. He asked again, "It is obvious this man was stoned by a group of people. I want to know who did it and why." Titus waited for an answer. Still, no one said anything.

Titus motioned to his men to surround the people. He addressed the small group of people, "If no one speaks, I will arrest all of you." The people realized they were trapped. All of them started talking at once. The authoritative voice of Titus rang out, "Stop! Just one person is to talk. I will let all of you go if I hear the truth."

One older man began, "Please, sir, we are afraid. We do not want to be arrested or get any of our people arrested."

"I understand that. Whether I arrest anyone or not depends on what I hear."

"No one here was involved. This man was stoned by the Priests and Pharisees and the leaders of our religion. The man was charged with blasphemy. Being guilty of blasphemy requires death by stoning in our religion."

Titus looked at the man intently, searching his eyes. He felt the man had told him the truth, so he said to the soldiers, "Let them go." The people hurried away in every direction. Titus went directly to the temple and asked to see the chief priest. Caiaphas, the high priest, came out.

Titus said, "I was told that you and others stoned a man. Is that true?"

"Yes, it is. The man blasphemed God and the Sanhedrin. That is a sin punishable by death in our laws."

"I don't know about your laws, but I know Roman law. You Jews are not allowed to impose the death penalty on anyone. You must know that as well."

"I must confess I do. In this case the stoning occurred in the heat of passion for our beliefs. The man deserved it. It is not something that we practice because of Roman law. That is why we took Jesus to Pilate."

"Since you knowingly broke the law, why should I not arrest you?"

"If you arrest me for this act, you must also arrest all members of the Sanhedrin and many temple leaders. That would leave the Jewish people without spiritual leadership, and it would cause all sorts of problems and wide spread unrest."

Titus was not ready for that answer, but he knew the high priest was right in what he said. "What you say is true. I have no desire to start an uproar, nor can I leave your people without leaders. Chaos could result. I have no choice. You may go."

Caiaphas responded, "Centurion, we leaders have no quarrel with Rome. Our quarrel is with a small group that is trying to destroy our beliefs. They are the followers of Jesus."

Titus asked, "Can you tell me their names?"

"There is one that is named Peter and another is named John. Those two I know for certain."

"Where can I find them?"

"I don't know. If I did, I would tell you."

"I will find them and talk to them."

"You will find them to be trouble makers."

Titus thought, "They may or may not be trouble makers but if I find them, they can tell me about the man Jesus."

He instructed his soldiers to search for Peter and John and anyone identified as a follower of Jesus. Each time a tip was received about someone's location, they were gone by the time the soldiers arrived. Twice the Pharisees sent word to Titus that Peter and John had gone into the temple. Each time soldiers waited outside looking for the two to leave but since they did not know what they looked like, so no one was stopped. Both men left the temple without being stopped. Finally, reports slowed to a trickle. Most of Jesus' followers left the city because of fear of being arrested.

Titus was frustrated. His chance to learn about the man called Jesus was vanishing. The day came when the replacement for Marcus arrived, and Titus could return to Caesarea.

He went homeward a changed man. On the way he thought about the information he had been given by Marcus along with what he had learned earlier from other sources. His belief in a plurality of gods was shaken. Many questions racked his brain. Could it be there was only one god? Was this man Jesus the son of the one god? If this is true, then why did he allow himself to be killed? There were now so many questions in his mind. Was there some meaning in all this, and if so, what? Would he ever have any answers?

As he traveled, the thought of seeing his family replaced the burning desire to find out about Jesus. He suddenly realized how much he had missed them. His mind returned to focusing on his family.

XII

A Man Called Peter

When Titus arrived in Caesarea, he reported to Emericus everything that had happened in Jerusalem, including the Pharisees claim that the followers of Jesus were trouble makers. He said he could sympathize with Marcus after being in Jerusalem for a few days. Then he asked about Marcus.

Emericus said, "He is some place in Rome if he is still alive. He had a death wish."

"Do you know if he is being cared for?"

"No, I don't. He was no longer classified as capable, so he was discharged from the army."

Titus felt his stomach turn over at the news. He thought Marcus should have been cared for because of his past service to Rome. He felt that being discharged was not fair to Marcus. He said to himself, "Is this the way the army takes care of its own? Their attitude is, if you can't or won't support our purpose, you are of no use to us."

Emericus got Titus's focus back on the situation in Jerusalem by asking, "Do you think the followers of Jesus are trouble makers?"

"No, I don't. I think the Jewish religious leaders hated Jesus so much that they wanted to destroy not only him but everything and everybody associated with him."

"Why do you say that?"

"I base it on the conversations I had with people in Jerusalem and what Ludo told me a year ago. Jesus encouraged peace and even told people to obey Roman rule. The role of troublemaker just does not fit that teaching."

Emericus replied, "Based on what you are telling me, I tend to believe there is no thought of a revolt in Jerusalem. Nor does it appear that any action is necessary on this Jesus group. If you learn anything to the contrary, I'll reconsider action. In the meantime, you deserve some time away from the army. Go spend time with your family and return in a week."

"Yes sir!" With that Titus rushed out and headed home. All else was forgotten. He didn't even look for Primus.

Drusilla had received word of Titus's return and was waiting for him in front of their home. When she saw him, she ran toward him, greeting him with warm embraces and kisses. Titus greeted her the same way. They stood in front of their house locked in each other's arms until they realized they were attracting a lot of attention.

"Come inside. I know you want to see the children."

Titus picked up Alexius and rubbed his head. "My but I think you have grown 50 centimeters." Alexius laughed but soon wanted down. Titus obliged the request. He wanted to hold his little daughter. Drusilla brought Adela and placed her in Titus's arms. He said, "She looks like you, Drusilla. She is the prettiest baby in all of the empire."

Drusilla said, "Oh, how you have changed!"

"What do you mean?" asked Titus.

"Don't you remember when Alexius was a baby? You would not touch him for fear of breaking him."

"Well, I have learned," he said with a smile. "Babies are fairly sturdy. They don't break."

Drusilla said, "Alexius missed you. He kept asking when you would be home, and I wanted to know the answer to that question as well."

"Drusilla, I know you did not understand when I left, but it was necessary for me to go. There was no leadership in Jerusalem, and the possibility of an uprising could have developed."

"I know it was important now. Primus kept me informed and helped me understand why you were needed there and could not be here."

Titus wanted to change the subject so he asked, "Has anything developed between Primus and Livia?"

Drusilla said, "He is still coming to see Livia, but nothing appears to be happening. They both seem to like each other, so I wonder what is missing. Do you think it could be because they are older than most marrying people or possibly because Livia was married once before?"

"I have no idea. I'll talk to Primus about Livia's previous marriage. He knows she has no husband, but he may not know why."

"Be tactful in what you say."

Titus was a little surprised by that statement, "Why did you say that?"

Drusilla said, "My father was always pressuring me about marriage, and I don't want Primus to think he is being pressured. Now tell me, what was Jerusalem like?"

"It is a city like other cities except it is larger than Caesarea, and it is the center of the Jewish religion, so there is a lot of activity." The words, *Jewish religion*, jolted Titus' memory and caused him to pause. Memories of wondering how land came into existence, when he was a youth. Then of the conversation with Primus when they were on the boat. He recalled Ludo's stories and what Marcus had told him. He had to stop and admit something to himself. The pause was long enough that Drusilla wondered if something was wrong.

"Titus, what is it that is bothering you?"

He answered, "Drusilla, because of what I learned while I was in Jerusalem and Ludo's stories, I have come to believe the Jews are right. There are not multiple gods. There is only one God, and he is all powerful. There are just too many things that have happened that are totally beyond human control, to believe otherwise. Only some great power could have caused them."

"Titus there still could be more than one god. But only one god that exercised his power. Did you think about that?"

"I did. I even told myself that was the explanation. I thought the healing of sick people could have been by Juno. The raising of dead people maybe by Jupiter. But which god caused the darkness and earthquake? I could not get that to fit using our gods. The more I thought about it, the more I always came back to the belief in only one God."

"I think you have felt that way for some time, Titus. But it was difficult for you to accept that idea."

"Maybe you are right. I think I started to wonder about it after talking with centurion Ludo. But enough of that talk for now."

They retired early that night but Titus slept little. His mind kept returning to the questions about Jesus and who he was. He kept trying to put the pieces of the puzzle together.

The morning sun woke them, Titus returned to the conversation of the previous evening. "Drusilla, I don't know where Jesus fits in, but I am convinced the Jews are a special group of people and deserve respect. I am not going to look down on them any longer or treat them as I have been doing."

"I don't think you have been mistreating them."

"Maybe not, but I have not accepted them as equals or shown them any respect. From now on, I will."

After a few months of pondering all that happened with Centurion Marcus, Titus began a series of restless nights ending with a dream, that frightened him. He had never dreamed much before. He ignored the dream, and said nothing about it. The following night he had the same dream. He sat up in bed and woke Drusilla.

"I just had the strangest dream for the last two nights. I don't know what to make of it."

"What was it about?" she asked as she tried to wake up.

"In my dream a winged creature with the face of a man flew to me and said God had noticed my attitude change, and then he told me to send someone to Joppa to get a man called Peter to come here and talk to me."

"Besides a man's face what else did you notice about this creature?"

"There was such a bright light around it that I could not tell. I do remember seeing wings and a face but that is about all."

"Did this creature talk to you about one of the gods?"

"It was the God of the Jews."

"That sounds bizarre, and who is Peter? Is that someone you have met?"

"No, I have never met anyone named Peter. And I am not certain who the man could be. There is a follower of Jesus by that name. I tried very hard to find him when I was in Jerusalem, but never located him. That is the only Peter I have ever heard about."

"Titus, I think your obsession of finding out who Jesus was has returned. That is why you had that dream. Clear your mind and try to go back to sleep."

"You are probably right. I am sorry I woke you up. Try to go back to sleep yourself." They both laid back down, but Titus could not sleep. He kept thinking about the dream.

Titus began treating Jews with more respect and compassion than he had in the past. Now he would not let any of his men abuse any Jew no matter what the circumstances. He would even give coins to the Jewish beggars on the streets.

The dream came back a third time and with more detail. He woke Drusilla again. "I just had the same dream. This time the creature told me not only the city but whose house to find Peter in. There is some spirit telling me to talk with Peter. I can feel it; otherwise, why do I keep having this same dream?"

Dursilla answered, "Maybe the gods are talking to you. I have heard that has happened to some people, but I never believed it."

"There has to be a reason. I just don't know what it is. I am going to send Primus to Joppa, to find Peter. If he finds Peter and brings him back here, then I will know some non-human power is involved."

Titus told Primus about his dream and asked him to go to Joppa and find a man called Peter. Primus rolled his eyes and thought Titus might be crazy. But he said, "I will go only because you asked me. I will lead a patrol there and check on what might be happening in the area."

"Thank you."

When Primus arrived in Joppa, he found the house owned by a man named Simon, which is where Titus had said he would find Peter. He called out from in front of the house, "I am looking for a man named Peter. If he is in the house, he should come out. Otherwise I will go in and search for him."

Primius made his proclamation sound like a threat. He hoped that would get an immediate response. Much to his amazement it did, a man walked out accompanied by some other men. "What do you want of me?"

"Are you Peter?"

"Yes, I am. Am I under arrest?"

"No, centurion Cornelius wants to talk with you. He has been having dreams that tell him to send for you. Will you go back to Caesarea with me?"

Peter hesitated for a minute, then said, "If a dream is the reason you were searching for me, I see God's providence is directing us. For I, too, had a strange dream which I did not understand. I was told in my dream to go with you. I am beginning to understand my dream now. Yes, I will go. I would like for my friends here to go with me. Will that be agreeable?"

"I think so. I would like to start back as soon as possible."

"We can go now if you wish, but you must provide for us since we have not prepared anything for a journey."

"Good. I will provide for your needs. Do you have anything you want to take?"

"No, just my friends."

After a two-day walk, they arrived at Titus' house. He saw them coming, and he felt a chill go down his spine. At that point he knew the one and only God was directing events. But why? Maybe he could get an answer from Peter. He went out to meet and greet them, "Welcome, which one of you is Peter?"

"I am Peter," answered the tallest man. Titus looked at Peter and said, "I searched for you all over Jerusalem but could not find you."

"I know, I was always warned and moved before you would arrive where I had been staying."

"Why did you run?"

"I didn't run, but I was afraid you would imprison me so I would leave."

"You did not need to be afraid; I just wanted to talk. I have wanted to talk to you for a long time. Are you afraid now?"

"God removed all thoughts of fear. I know we are meeting at God's direction. If there is danger for me, God will control the outcome."

Titus smiled, "You have nothing to fear. I was told to send for you in a dream. The dream even told me the house where you are staying. I meant it when I said you are welcome in my home, and my family would like to meet you as well. I want my family to hear what you have to say. They are willing to come outside because we know you are not supposed enter into our homes."

Peter said, "Of course I will speak to your family. But do not concern yourself with our religious rules. Our rule was established to keep us from unclean things. And God has shown me that it is wrong to think some people are unclean. I will go inside with you. Your family will be more comfortable inside rather than out here in the hot sun."

Peter's friends were surprised at what he said. One whispered, "I have followed Peter's teaching since he baptized me. So, even though I don't understand, I will follow his example." Titus said, "That is thoughtful of you; let's do go inside."

After they were inside Titus called for Drusilla, Livia, and Coto to join them. He also asked Primus to come in and listen. He told Primus,

"After all, you are almost part of my family." Primus choked. Titus smiled and whispered. "Later I want to ask you a question."

When they all were seated comfortably, Peter began, "Centurion, Titus, Cornelius, how should I address you?"

"Whatever you prefer will be all right."

"Since we have just met, Cornelius would be appropriate. So, Cornelius, I have been told you want to know who Jesus was. I will tell you because God has opened my eyes so that I can see He is reaching out to all people and not just us Jews."

Titus was surprised by that comment and said, "Peter, I thought that your God was only for Jews. Now I hear you say, He is God to everybody, even us Romans."

"Yes, that is true. I would have not told you that a year ago, but Yahweh is much greater than I thought. I, too, have things to learn. Now, your question about Jesus. Jesus was and is the Son of God. I was with him for three years and saw him do amazing things during that time. But that is not what is important. What is important is why he came into the world. Through his coming, we could be forgiven for our sins and live forever with Him in heaven. Jesus knew from his birth why he was here, and he knew when and how he would die. He died willingly and his body was placed in a tomb, but he rose from the tomb and is alive today."

Titus looked confused. "I don't understand what you are saying. What do you mean by sins and why do we need to be saved from them? And this heaven, is it a city or a country? And wherever it is; and how do we get there?"

"Forgive me, I have exposed you to many new concepts. It is a lot to take in at one time. I'll start over by asking you a question. Do you know how the world was created?"

Titus replied, "I never thought much about it. I wondered about that when I was a young fellow but was told, it has always existed. I have always accepted that explanation."

"No, it has not always existed. God created it and everything in it. He even created the first man and woman and put them into a garden that was perfect in every way. The pair could do anything they wanted except for one thing. The one thing they were not to do, they did. They yielded to temptation that was too strong for them to resist. Their temptation was desiring something that God had specifically said they could not have. They disobeyed.

"Their act of disobedience was doing what God told them not to do, and that terribly disappointed Him. Anything that we do that disappoints God or detracts from his Holiness is a sin. So, the first couple sinned. The result of their sin was a curse that separated them from God. This curse has been passed down to every man and woman through every generation since.

"When we are born, we begin in life tainted by this handed down sin. Then as we live, we are tempted by pleasures and desires that we many times act upon. When we do, we are disappointing

God; we have committed another sin. God has told us that sin is not acceptable to Him and will be punished by another death. So, if the sin is not forgiven then living in heaven with God will not happen. The person lives on but without God, and this places him in total darkness. This is eternal death."

Drusilla asked, "What do you mean by eternal death?"

"When most people think of death, they see a person who is no longer breathing. That is an earthly death. But it is not the end. There is life after earthly death but not in this world or in the same manner as earthly life. That life will take place in one of two places. One is in heaven with God and Jesus; the other is in a total darkness of despair, completely separated from God and Jesus. This separation from God and staying in darkness is the eternal death."

Titus asked, "Are you saying when you are dead you are not really dead?"

"I guess you could say it that way. After a person breathes his last breath here, he will face God who will decide if he can live in His kingdom or go into darkness forever."

Primus said," You have not explained heaven yet. Is heaven and God's Kingdom the same thing?"

Peter answered, "You can think of it that way. Consider heaven as a place where Jesus, God and all people who have put their faith in them, will be together. I like to think of it being like that perfect garden where the first man and woman lived. But that is just my idea. I'll talk more about this later."

No one said anything more. It was momentarily quiet. All were trying to absorb what Peter had said.

Drusilla was the first to speak, she asked, "Is that what happened to that first man and that woman? Did they die and go into that darkness?"

Peter answered, "No, they did not die at that time. They remained in this world. But after the first man and woman sinned,

God made them leave the garden where he had met with them. He is righteous and holy. He will not tolerate the existence of sin near His person. In fact, in God's world, sin is punishable by death. This means by God's standards; everyone deserves death since all of us are tainted with sin.

"I'll say again, God is holy and He abhors sin. People who are tainted with sin are in jeopardy of His righteous judgment. Yet God loves people and wants to have a relationship with people.

"How does he resolve his desire to be with people yet not have sin near Him? There is only one answer. Something or somebody must satisfy the death requirement that each of us has. Otherwise, every one of us would go into that darkness where there is no hope."

Titus said, "I don't see how death and sin are connected. Your God's world sounds the same as ours. If a person is guilty of an offense that requires death, they die. And how can one person die for another person? I know a lot of people and none of them had someone die for them. They all just kept living the same way until they died."

"Titus, you are talking about death from a human point of view. I am not talking about what happens during our walk on this earth. I am talking about what happens after you breathe your last breath. Remember I said there is life in heaven or a life in darkness. That is the eternal life that follows this one. The life in heaven is given to the followers of God while people that reject God by their continual sinning receive the life in darkness. Do I need to say more?"

"Yes, please do."

Peter thought for a minute then asked, "Do you accept that God has decreed that sin must be paid for by death?"

Slowly heads began to nod in an affirmative way.

He continued, "Think of how many people have lived before us. They all sinned. If all their sins were added together, that would be a huge number and what would balance out that number? I'll ask another way, could there be a death that would equal all of those people's deaths?"

The small group looked at one another and finally Titus said, "the number of people that lived before me is larger than I could imagine. If you are looking for one thing that would balance all of those people's deaths, it would need to be enormous and special."

Peter said, "Yes, it would; the only thing that fits the requirement is God himself. Even though God is holy and just, He is also merciful. God wanted to provide that death requirement in a way that man could understand. So, he lowered himself to us in the form of a human baby and entered this world the same way you and I came into the world. He lived a life like all other people live, but without sinning. That baby was named Jesus."

Titus' eyes lit up, "So that is who Jesus was. That is why he could do the things he did. He was this God."

"Yes! As I said, Jesus lived just like anyone else in this world, only in a perfect manner. He never sinned.

"He taught me and many others about his Father God and explained how God wanted us to live. Yet God knew we could not do so. He still wanted us with him and so he willingly let himself be arrested and killed in a horrible way to pay for our sin debt requirement. Because of his sacrificing himself, we are given the opportunity to spend forever with him in heaven after we take our last breath here on earth and not be in that eternal darkness. The only thing that God requests we do to accept this opportunity, is to acknowledge our submission to Jesus as our Savior and Master, and repent of our sins."

"You say 'we' as if it applies to Romans as well as Jews. Is that true?"

"I would have answered no, until a few days ago. Now, I say Yahweh can be your God as well as mine, and He is inviting you to be with Him in His heaven."

Peter's friends interrupted, "Peter how can this be?"

Peter responded, "Yahweh corrected my thinking by the dreams Cornelius and I had."

Then he turned toward Titus and said, "It is now clear to me that God has brought us together. You told me about your dream. I will tell you about mine. In my dream I saw all kinds of animals, what to us are clean and unclean animals. I was told to eat some of everything there. I balked. I was not going to eat anything unclean! That would have been wrong to my way of thinking. I was taught all my life not even to touch anything unclean. But God told me, 'Don't you call anything I have made unclean.' I could not understand what he was telling me until I came here. He was telling me not to think of people as being clean or unclean. Instead accept that all peoples can become part of God's family and are included in his plan of salvation. It is not just for the Jewish people.

At that moment a bright light filled the room and a strong wind swept through the house. Cornelius and the Romans in the room quivered as if cold water had been thrown in their face. One of Peter's friends said, "It is the Holy Spirit. How can this be?" It lasted only momentarily. The room became normal again. Peter and his Jewish friends began praising God.

Cornelius knew something special had happened, but he was not certain what had happened. Suddenly his heart had a yearning that was seeking answers to fill an internal emptiness that had started after his first exposure to Jesus. Yet there was a calmness he had never known before that flooded his mind. The words, "listen to Peter" were whispered in his ear. He was experiencing a new environment and wanted this feeling to last forever. However, with his past life history, he thought the feeling would only be temporary. He looked intently at Peter and asked, "So, you are telling me, I can be included as a follower of Jesus and live forever even though I have done some dreadful things and have not lived a life that meets God's standards?"

"Yes, Titus. God has just confirmed that by his presence just now."

"Peter, you don't know some of the terrible things I have done, and I am certainly not going to talk about them now."

"Titus, it is not what you have done in the past, it is what you do from this moment forward into the future that is important. You can spend eternity with Him if you surrender to Him, accept Him as your Lord and Savior, and truly are sorry for the sins in your life, and repent and be baptized just as Jesus wants us to do."

Titus said, "I like the thought of living eternally with Jesus; however, I hear the word submit rather than surrender and you used the word, submit, before. I have trouble with the thought of submitting to anybody. I experienced submission twice in my past life, and I'm not sure I want to do that again."

Peter reassured him, "I don't know the submission circumstances of your past, but I do know this. Submission to Christ is not confining; it is liberating. In fact, in some ways you will find a freedom you never experienced before. This creates a desire in your heart to serve God and His people. Don't think of submission to God as inhibiting you. Yes, it is a commitment to follow Him but it is fulfilling. By making this commitment you will be blessed in many ways."

"This submission appears to be different than the way I always defined submission before. You do sound convincing, and I have an emptiness that I feel Jesus would fill. Maybe I should not let the word, submission, hold me back from accepting Jesus as Lord."

"It is different. You will be serving, but it will provide you joy. When you share your testimony and people respond by accepting Christ, you will see changed lives. What a joy that will bring to you. When you visit or assist someone who is experiencing difficulties or sickness, you will see the gratitude on their face and that moment enlightens your heart. No. Don't let your old thoughts about submission hold you back."

Titus said, "I have never thought about serving other people. Serving people was a task for slaves. That will be a new experience for me."

Livia asked, "I know what repenting means. What do you mean by baptized?"

"Baptism is immersion of the whole body under water. It is a representation of your death to sin as you go under water. Then your being raised from the water represents your being raised from the grave into a new life in Jesus Christ, just as Jesus was raised from the grave after his crucifixion."

Drusilla said, "So this is a task we must do to be with Jesus."

Peter shook his head, "No. Don't think of baptism as a task that you must do. Think of it as you are publicly announcing your acceptance and commitment to Jesus to everybody. It is not the emersion under water that counts. It is what happens within you at the time of baptism. The emersion of your heart and soul into a new life. It is a baptism by the Spirit of God."

Primus asked, "you said Jesus was raised from his grave. Does that mean that people really did see Jesus after his death?"

"Oh, yes I not only saw Jesus and talked with him, I ate with him. The last time I saw him, a group of us were walking up a hill with him when he stopped. He looked at us in a way I will never forget and said, "Go all over the world and tell people about me." Then he started rising up into the sky. The higher he went, a light around him became brighter and brighter. We watched until he disappeared into the clouds. I was so overcome with emotion that I could not move. I just kept looking up into the sky. Suddenly two heavenly beings stood beside us and said, "Jesus will return to earth the same way he left. Don't just stand here. Go and tell people about Jesus Christ."

The room was filled with silence as each person appeared to be picturing Jesus rising into the clouds.

"Titus from the moment you truly accept, Jesus Christ as you Lord and Savior, He considers you a member of his family and will wrap his arms around you and accept you into his kingdom. Your place in heaven is assured after your life here on earth ends."

"Peter, when I connect what you are telling us to what others have told me and my experiences in Jerusalem, it fills my emptiness and I am wanting more. I don't want to spend time in that eternal darkness. I want to be a member of God's family. I accept Jesus as my Lord and Savior. Will you baptize me?"

"Yes, I will. We can go to the sea to do it."

Titus turned to Drusilla and asked, "Do you feel the need to accept Jesus and be baptized as I do?"

Drusilla answered, "I have never heard about a life after death before, and I don't want to spend that time in darkness. I want to be in God's world with you. But I need to learn more about Jesus."

Livia said, "I have never heard anyone talk like you, Peter. I don't understand all you have said. I do understand the part about a life lasting forever and I would like to have that with God. Could I be baptized as well?"

Peter smiled and said, "You do not need to have all the answers to accept Jesus Christ. You only need to believe and have faith."

Coto looked at Peter and asked, "Can a slave be included?"

Peter said, "Most certainly, all people includes slaves. Everyone is equal in God's eyes."

All eyes turned toward Primus who said, "After listening to you, Peter, I believe that Jesus was the son of the true and only God. I also wished to be baptized."

Drusilla's slave who had been with the children walked into the room and said, "I heard what you have been talking about. Can I be included?"

Peter said, "Yes you can. Come and join us."

They left Titus' house with Titus holding Alexius' hand and Drusilla carrying Adela. As they walked to the sea, two of Peter's friends quietly said, "Peter, these people must convert to Judaism before they can be baptized."

"No, they don't need to. That is what God was showing me in my dream. God's invitation to be in His family is meant for all peoples. Also, I can see that Titus' dream was an invitation from God to join his family. Besides, the Holy Spirit that we just witnessed was giving His approval. So, there is no requirement to convert to Judaism before they are baptized."

When they reached the seashore, Peter and Titus walked out into the water until they were waist deep. Then Peter turned to Titus and said, "Titus, do you believe that Jesus is the son of God and are you willing to accept him as your Lord and Savior?"

Titus answered "Yes. I believe he is God's son and I know he is my savior." and Peter baptized him. Then, in turn, Peter baptized Drusilla, Livia, the two slaves, and Primus after asking each one, if they believed that Jesus is the son of God and they accepted him as their Lord and Savior. After all of them were baptized, Peter prayed for God to bless Primus, Titus and all those in his household. He asked God to keep the evil one away from them, and, to use them to reach other people.

As they walked back, people who saw them wondered if there had been a boating accident since all of them were soaking wet. The wet group felt a different kind of cleanliness than from any previous bath. They all thanked Peter for bringing God's message to them. Primus added, "We would never have known about the true God and what He has in mind for us if you had not told us."

Peter responded, "A 'thank you' is not necessary. I am only doing what Jesus told me to do. I encourage all of you to tell others what you have learned."

XIII

A New Life

By the time they had reached home, it was late in the day. Drusilla spoke first, "Peter, I know so little. Will you stay with us for a few days and teach us about Jesus and life after death?"

Coto joined in, "I want to know more as well."

Titus added, "We all want to learn more about Jesus. I hope you will stay."

Peter answered, "I will gladly stay for two or three days. I will begin tomorrow. Right now, I would like to be alone to spend some time in prayer. I want to thank God for making His will clear to me. I understand now because He directed me to you, and He allowed me the privilege of baptizing all of you."

One of Peter's friends said, "Peter, I must go home. I have some duties to attend to, and you do not appear to be in any danger."

Another friend said, "We are not required here, God is in control. I, too, should leave this evening as well."

Livia said, "You are welcome to spend the night here then leave in the morning."

"You are kind, but there is still some daylight and we can go part of the way before darkness overtakes us."

Drusilla added, "Please do not leave until we can prepare a meal for you." They agreed.

Drusilla and Livia quickly prepared a meal for everyone. When all had finished eating, Peter's friends left with food to sustain them on their journey. Peter went to find a place to be alone. Titus' family and Primus discussed what had taken place that day. All agreed there was an inner feeling of peace that they had never felt before.

Coto, who had been quiet all through dinner said, "I want to thank everyone for allowing me to join you in your evening meal. If I am not being too bold, you made me feel like I was part of your family."

Livia said, "Coto, Peter told us today we are all equal. It seems to me that makes you part of the family of God just like us, so, we are brother and sister."

Titus added, "Coto, I'm not sure how to make it official while we are in Judea, but you are no longer a slave as far as I am concerned. You are free to leave, or you are welcome to stay."

"Thank you for saying that. I will continue serving you if I may."

"If that is what you want, we are pleased - only do not consider yourself a servant."

This type of relationship was new to Coto and he said so, then he added, "I have one other concern. I would like to do something for Peter to show my thanks for telling me about Jesus, but I don't know how to do that."

Primus said, "Coto, I don't think Peter expects or wants any thanks. You could just say, God bless, or God be with you." He stopped. A thought occurred to him and he said," It never occurred to me that Peter would feel threatened when I brought him here until I heard one of his friends say 'You do not appear to be in any danger'. Now I realize that is why they came with Peter."

Titus said, "Primus, you are probably right. They must have thought they were going to be arrested and imprisoned. We all know what I wanted was to talk to Peter about Jesus. He obviously did not know that. I am grateful that everything turned out all right."

"So am I." declared Primus, then he thanked the ladies for a fine meal and started to leave, Titus said, "I'll walk out with you." When the two were outside, Titus said, "Primus, you obviously have strong feelings for Livia because you have been coming to see her for some time. Yet, the subject of marriage has never been mentioned. Is it because she has been married before?"

"Not at all. I asked centurion Emericus for permission to marry Livia, but he said no. That is why I never brought up the subject of marriage. I knew it could not happen."

"Did he say why?"

"There were two reasons, first, was having two married officers in one centuria. He had never heard or seen that before, and he didn't think it would be a very good example. Secondly, He said marrying your sister would make our relationship too close and personal. That could possibly jeopardize our centuria if one of us ever made a poor decision in a critical situation because of a close relationship."

"I'll talk to Emericus and see if I can get him to change his mind."

The next morning after they had eaten, Titus said to Peter, "There are some military duties that I must perform, and then I will be back. If you want to go ahead and talk to my wife and sister that will be all right." As he started to leave, Coto got up to go with him. He said to Coto, "Coto, why don't you stay and listen to Peter. Remember you are no longer a servant. I have always appreciated your service, but you do not need to go to the fortress with me."

"Thank you, sir. I would have left with you. Habits are hard to break."

One of the things Titus had in mind was to talk to Emericus about Primus's request to marry. As soon as he got to the fortress, he went to Emericus and said, "Primus Constant told me he requested permission to marry my sister, but you refused, stating such a marriage would create too close of a relationship between us."

Emericus replied, "That is correct. I have nothing against Constant. I told him I had never seen or heard of two married officers in a centuria and secondly, I was concerned that the relationship created by such a marriage might possibly weaken decisions made in a war situation."

"I see your point Emericus, but remember both Constant and I are veterans of the German campaigns. We know what is required to win battles. The relationship between us will not change if Constant marries my sister. We both realize duty comes first. Also, we both will honor the oath we took when we entered the army. As for having two married officers in the same centuria, I don't know of another example either, but is there a rule that would forbid it? Or, really is that a valid reason to deny a marriage? I am asking you to reconsider your decision."

Emericus accepted Titus' comments and seem to be weighing them in his mind. After a few moments of silence he said, "Good points. I had forgotten both of you had an outstanding record in the German wars. Plus, you have made good decisions in matters since you have been here. As for my other concern, I suppose you could be right. Just because there is not a centuria with two married officers, does not mean there could not be one. So, I will reconsider Constant's request, but I still have a concern. I will send for him."

"He is waiting outside."

Emericus smiled, "Bring him in. I have one question for him."

Primus came in and saluted. Emericus asked, "Constant, if you were in a battle and had to make a decision that would increase the danger to centurion Cornelius but save the lives of 20 men, whom would you choose to save?"

Without looking at Titus, Primus responded without hesitation, "I would save the 20 men."

"Well said Constant. That is what I wanted to hear. You have my permission to get married."

Primus had a large smile on his face and said, "Thank you, sir!" The two men left and started toward Titus' home.

Meanwhile Titus's family was engaged in questioning Peter about the kingdom of God. Drusilla asked, "Peter, after I come back to life again, will I still be in Judea or will I be back in Italia?"

Peter smiled and answered, "I am not sure you will be in either place."

"Then where will I be?"

"I cannot tell you for certain where you will be, but I do know this. You will be wherever God and Jesus Christ are. Jesus never gave us a specific location when he talked about God's kingdom. In fact he told me one time, I could not follow him there."

Perplexed Drusilla asked, "Is this some sort of mystery we are supposed to figure out?"

"No, the location of heaven is not what is important. Try not to think of heaven as a physical place that you could stand on. Instead, think about an area like a cloud. Remember I said before that heaven and the Kingdom of God were the same. It is perfect in every way and Jesus is king of the kingdom!"

Livia asked, "But Peter, if we don't know where heaven is located, then we won't know how to get there."

"Do not be concerned. Jesus will lead those who are his followers into His kingdom. Instead of the location of heaven, focus on who is there and what awaits there for us. That is what is important."

"I know God and Jesus will be there but what waits for us?"

"Well, all the people that put their faith in Jesus as God's son are there. You and I have a spot waiting for us there and we will see Jesus, face to face. Then there will be more than you could imagine. I'll tell of the things I do know that will be there. First, there will be singing, praising, and glorifying God in worship. As for us, Jesus told us there will be no more pain or tears, no war or troubles, and there will be a peace that exceeds anything we have ever known. We will get new bodies which will never deteriorate like the ones we have now. We will never have sorrows or experience painful conditions. There will be more. I just do not know what it will be."

The ladies and Coto kept asking questions and Peter patiently answered them until about mid-day, when Titus returned with Primus, who still had a big grin on his face. Primus rushed over to where Livia was sitting, raised her up and kissed her. She was not only surprised, she was embarrassed. Primus held on to her saying, "I have your brother's and my commander's permission to marry you. I want to marry you right now unless you say no."

Livia's reply was immediate. "I have been waiting for you to ask me that for a long time. Yes! I do want to marry you."

Primus released Livia, turned and asked, "Peter, is there a wedding ceremony for the marriage of Jesus' followers?"

Peter replied, "That is one question I have never been asked. I'll have to say no. However, we Jews always had a priest perform a marriage ceremony. I think that is a good practice to continue even for the followers of Jesus."

"We consider you as our priest. Will you marry us?"

Peter was surprised at Primus' request. "I never thought about marrying people. I baptize them so I suppose I could perform a marriage ceremony. Let me think about it."

Suddenly a concerned Livia said, "Primus, I do not have a dowry that our custom entitles you to. I am sorry."

Primus replied, "A dowry is not important to me."

Titus said, "Drusilla and I will provide for all the furnishings needed in your home, and I will ask Fishel to find you a place to live."

Primus told Livia, "Your brother's gift offer is better than a dowry wouldn't you say?"

Livia laughed and said, "Thank you, Drusilla and Titus. This is very kind of you. Now I must make preparations for our wedding."

Primus said, "Livia we don't need any preparations if we marry now." He turned to Peter and asked, "Peter, have you decided how to marry people?"

Peter answered, "I am ready, if you two are. I can only provide a simple ceremony so let's begin. Will Livia and Primus face me? The rest of you are witnesses to what is about to take place."

He placed Livia's hand between Primus' two hands and said, "I believe God intended for a man and woman to marry when he first put Adam and Eve together in the garden he created. It will be He that truly marries the two of you. For that reason, I am willing to assist in your desire to marry. First, do you both truly love one another? Before you answer, remember God is among us and is listening."

Livia and Primus answered together, "Yes".

"Do you both agree to respect your pledge of love forever, no matter what the circumstances in your lives are?"

Again, they both gave an affirmative answer.

"Are you both willing to include God in all you do?"

Primus responded, "He is part of our lives now."

Livia answered, "Yes!"

Peter continued, "I do not know what the Roman government's requirements are for marriage, but I, and I am sure God, view the two of you as married. I will now ask God to bless your marriage." With that, Peter lowered his head and said, "Glorious God in heaven, we praise you for your holiness, and we thank you for your forgiveness. Just now I ask that you bless this man and woman who wish to be united as one. I pray they will always follow your guidance. May you be a part of their lives for evermore and lead them on the path of righteousness."

After all heads were raised, everyone's eyes looked toward the newlywed couple. As expected, Primus kissed Livia.

Titus and Drusilla gave them both a hug. Alexius, confused with this strange talk and ceremony asked, "What is going on?" Everyone laughed. "It is something you will understand when you grow up."

Peter said, "Let's sing and be joyful in the Lord. This is a special day! The Lord is here with us, and He must have a smile on His face."

"Peter, we don't know any song that would be appropriate."

"Then let me share something that was written many years ago by one of God's prophets. It goes like this 'Sing joyfully to the Lord, you righteous; it is fitting for the upright to praise him. Praise the Lord with the harp; make music to him on the ten-stringed lyre. Sing to him a new song; play skillfully, and shout for joy. For the word of the Lord is right and true'. I tell you this because I want you to know that God is a God of rejoicing, and I am sure he is rejoicing not only for this marriage but for all of you becoming part of his family. So, let us be joyful as well. Tomorrow we will talk about Jesus."

Titus said, "Coto, would you bring us some wine to celebrate this wedding."

Drusilla quickly said, "Titus, maybe we should not drink wine since we are now followers of Jesus." They both looked at Peter, expecting some direction.

Peter said, "Remember what I told you that was in my dream. God said, 'Do not call anything I have made unclean?' I believe he is telling us that anything that comes from his creation is all right for us to eat or drink. He had nothing against wine; in fact, the first miracle Jesus did was to turn water into wine at a wedding ceremony. What God does detest is drunkenness, and that he condemned as a sin."

There was a surprised look on faces when they heard drunkenness was a sin. Peter sensed there could be a fear of a lot of rules they would have to follow. He continued, "There are no 'do this and don't do that' rules that a follower must abide by. Just don't continue to follow the evil desires of your previous life. Your heart will tell you what is good or bad. The only thing I would suggest is, you just should not eat, drink or do anything in excess, unless it is to praise God."

The afternoon became a time of joy and celebration.

Titus left the house early the next morning. He wanted to fulfill his duties quickly and return to spend as much time as possible with Peter. Primus did not report until mid-morning. Titus told him, "I am going home to talk to Peter. When you have finished your tasks, come and join us."

Drusilla and Livia were sitting outside listening to Peter when Titus walked up. What he heard was questions about praying. Livia had asked if they should pray as Peter had yesterday.

Peter told her, "Don't repeat the same words I used, use your own words. Praying is just talking to God just like you are talking to me. Say whatever is on your mind. He will listen. You may make requests. Ask for His Spirit to lead you. Pray for other people who are in need.

"Jesus said, 'whatever you ask in my name, it will be granted'. He also said, 'you must believe and not doubt'".

Livia asked, "What does ask in my name mean?"

Peter answered, "Our requests should be in line with what God wants. They should not be of a self-serving nature."

Drusilla asked, "If we do ask for something, will God give us an answer?"

"If your prayer requires an answer from him, he will answer, but it will be when he wants to answer, not when we want to hear an answer. One suggestion I will make is begin your prayers by praising him. He is holy and righteous. He deserves praise."

XIV

Conviction

Titus sat down and asked, "Peter, will you tell us about the miracles Jesus performed?"

"His miracles are not what is important. He performed them to prove His deity, and also, to show His compassion for people with afflictions and illnesses. We should not focus just on miracles. Instead concentrate on Him and learning his ways. Jesus wants us to accept and follow Him and yet we live in this world of temptations.

"He knows what we face so he gives us guidance. Not a list of laws about what to do or don't do. He gave us guidelines he wants us to live by, through his words and the examples his actions created. His compassionate healing of people shows us we must have compassion for others. His words that instruct us to love God first and with all our heart; then next to love others, tells us he wants a relationship with us that will grow.

"It is a step-by-step process. Titus, consider your own experience. You never saw Jesus but you were told about him. Then you became obsessed with him, which developed into love for him. His Spirit touched your heart, and you accepted him. He in turn provided you with salvation."

Livia said, "Peter, I didn't have the obsession that Titus did, but yesterday I did know something had happened to me. I felt empty and wanted something to fill the emptiness."

Peter said to Livia, "What happened to you was a sudden urge to search for knowledge. Think about food and eating a meal. You tasted that the Lord is good, so you had a craving for the food of God. The food of God is the story of Jesus and God's desire for us to be part of his family. As you partake of this food, you discover it is good and you want more. If this is what you felt, you are growing in faith and knowledge. As you grow in faith and knowledge, you grow in your relationship with Jesus."

"Explaining it that way leads me to say, feed us, Peter."

Peter addressed all of them, "First of all as I said, Jesus instructed us to be loving. We should love God more than anything else. One of the ways we show that love is to bring glory to him in some way. What we do and say should glorify God. Whenever you have a decision to make, ask yourself which answer to my situation will bring glory to God.

"Next, we should love others, others mean everybody; this includes anyone you hate or is an enemy. That is difficult, but with God's help it can be done. If you forget all I say today try to remember this point. Jesus wants us to express our love to others by sharing our material things and our money with others who are in need and by serving one another when there is need. Jesus set the example of serving at the last meal I had with him before he was crucified. He washed everyone's feet. I could not believe it when he started doing it. I didn't understand until much later. Most of all he wants us to pass on to others his message of forgiveness and salvation."

Coto asked, "This is the second time you have said salvation. What do you mean by salvation, Peter?"

"The simple answer is being saved from your sins. The question then becomes, how? Remember, I told you how all people had inherited a sin nature from the first couple? People live their lives with little or no understanding of their bent to sin. Hence, they commit many sins during their life. And God abhors sin and condemns it, so people who never change from their sinful ways will never be with God. They will eternally be in hopeless darkness. Other people who make a decision to change and chose to believe there is only one God, that Jesus Christ is his son, and that he came to earth as a human to save us, and they are willing to accept Him into their heart, will spend eternity with Him. These people are given an inheritance that is kept in heaven and can never be taken away. This is salvation."

"You are saying that everyone anywhere can become a follower of Jesus if they believe and accept him? There is no other requirement?"

"I'll repeat what I said two days ago. Anyone, anywhere who wants truly to be a follower of Jesus must repent from their sinful past, as well as submitting and accepting Jesus Christ as Savior. That is the only requirement. This salvation is a gift from God. A person cannot pay for it nor do anything to earn it."

About that time, Primus joined them, and Peter talked until dark about Jesus and what he had learned from him. Titus asked, "Peter, we Romans had never heard of Jesus. We did not know about God and His salvation. I think about all my men who have never known there is only one true God. I would like for all the men at the fortress to hear you. Will you stay one more day to tell them about Jesus and the true God?"

"Your concern for others is good evidence of your desire to follow Jesus. Bless you, Cornelius. I was not planning to stay any longer, but to talk about Jesus to that many Romans at one time is an opportunity I cannot refuse. I will stay."

"Good, I will ask for permission from my superior in the morning for you to talk to them. I see no reason why he would not grant permission. As soon as he says yes, I will send word for you to come to the fortress."

Primus said, "Titus, that is a great idea. I hope it will be approved."

Early the next morning Titus made his request to Emericus. He said, "My family and I have been talking with Peter, a follower of Jesus. He is the man we were searching for. He is a peaceable and forgiving man. He impressed me to the point that I suggest he address the men here at the fortress. He has thought provoking information to share."

Emericus asked, "What is it that has impressed you so much about this man?"

"His mannerisms and the words he speaks seem to penetrate your heart. He has convinced me there is only one true God. The God the Jews talk about, only He is not just a God for the Jews. He is a God for all people. I am convinced that Jesus who was crucified by Marcus, really was the son of God."

Emericus' head jerked, "Stop right there, Cornelius! Did I hear you say there is only one god? You know we have many gods including Caesar, and he is the one we are required to revere. Then after him we can have whatever gods we want. I have even heard you say this before."

"I used to feel that way, but I now know that is not the truth. There is only one God who created this world." Titus realized there was a problem by the look on Emericus' face. He said, "I will continue to honor my oath to Rome, and accept Tiberius as Caesar. At the same time, I believe there is just one God. I do not consider Caesar a god. He is only an emperor. Peter can explain all this better than I."

Silence filled the room. Emericus kept looking at Titus. He turned away and said, "I am glad no one else is here to hear what you just said. I am going to forget what you just said. You have been a good officer for Rome, but your new belief does not fit in Rome's culture or what Caesar demands. You must know that."

"I do know that, but what Peter talks about is a culture that is so much better. Nothing needs to change except the concept of Caesar being a god. I will continue to obey all orders and protect Rome's interests as long as I am in the army."

Emericus turned back toward Titus and said, "Rome's culture is not going to be replaced. This man will not speak here, and if you keep talking about one God, it will put you in serious trouble; it could even result in your death. You must never speak like this again if you want to stay in the army. Otherwise, you must resign from the army. Those are your only choices."

Emericus was not comfortable with the conversation. He paused then said, "A year ago we had a conversation about retirement. You were eligible for retirement. I told you I would live my life out in the army and I hoped you would as well. You said time with your family was what was important to you and you were going to retire, but you would finish your tour here before retiring. If you resign now, you will lose your retirement."

Titus did not hesitate. "Sir I would like to finish this tour in the army, but I cannot go back to the Roman way of thinking there are many gods and that Caesar is one of them. If my belief in one God is not acceptable, then I have no choice but to resign."

"Do you realize that not only will you lose your retirement and receive no pay, you could even be placed on trial?"

"Yes sir, I do."

Emericus could not believe what was taking place. He looked at Titus for a long time before saying, "Very well, much to my disappointment I must say, as of this moment you are no longer considered a centurion. I will have the actarius prepare the papers this morning." Emericus paused again. He was struggling with what was transpiring, "Cornelius, you have served well. I hate to lose you, but your mind seems set so I will not ask you again to change your mind. However, I will tell you this; because of your past service, I will tell no one why you are leaving the army. If trouble comes your way, it will not have come from me."

"Thank you, sir."

"What will you do now?"

"I suppose I'll take my family back to Italia."

Both men stood looking at each other, neither spoke until Emericus said, "Cornelius, I will arrange ship's passage for you and your family back to Italia. You are entitled to that much."

"Thank you again, sir." There was no farewell greeting even though these two men who had been side by side for several years, parted. Titus turned and walked away. He never stopped to speak to Primus or to get anything belonging to him. He walked out from the gate and turned toward his home.

Primus was filling out the roster for sentry duty when one of his men said to him, "I just heard Cornelius has left the Army. Is that true?'

"That is ridiculous. Who is starting that rumor?"

"The actarius said he just filled out the papers."

Primus had just posted the roster when he was summoned. He was already planning on seeing Emericus.

Meanwhile, Titus reached home. He said to Peter, "I'm sorry, but Emericus will not accept the thought of only one God. Permission for you to speak was not granted. In fact, the belief in many gods is so engrained in army culture, the possibility of something different from multi god belief will not be considered. The belief in one all-powerful God is not acceptable to Emericus. I was expected to profess that Caesar was a god. I would not do that." He paused and took a deep breath, then he continued, "Because I would not renounce my belief in one God, the army felt my services were no longer required. I must leave."

A surprised Drusilla said, "Did I hear you say you are no longer in the army?"

"Yes, that is true. That was my only choice."

Drusilla didn't know what to say. She stood with a shocked look on her face and her mouth open.

Peter said, "Bless you! I am certain that was not what you wanted. However, you have demonstrated the strength of your faith. God will not forget what you have done."

Drusilla was trying to focus on what this might mean, "What will you do now? Will we stay here forever?"

"No, we will not be staying in Judea. Emericus said he would arrange passage for us back to Naples. As for what I will do now, I'm not sure. I may plant grapevines on that hector of land your father gave me when we got married. I learned about caring for grapevines from my father before I joined the army. I have accumulated enough money from my army pay and the spoils I took in the German wars to last us for a while. By then maybe we will have grapes to sell."

Peter said, "If that is your plan, I believe God will bless it. This could be what God wanted to have happen. He may want you to go to Italia to share your belief with others, and serve them"

"Sorry but I cannot see any connection between what I said and what God may want."

"Sometimes ideas that pop into our heads are put there by God. God can control events by methods we do not see. The connection could be a grapevine. The grapevine has been in our culture for many years. Past prophets wrote about the grapevine and how it is a representation of our nation's relationship with almighty God. Jesus made reference to it the night before His trial. He said, 'I am the true grapevine and my Father is the gardener.' Now, Titus, you are transplanting that grapevine in Italia. Through you, God will be reaching out to the Roman people. May the vines you plant be productive in both grapes and new believers in God's Kingdom."

"I would never have thought about it like you just said. If that is my task, I need help and a lot of prayers."

Peter said, "Prayers, I can and will give you but physical help I cannot do. God will be with you and He will provide the help"

Drusilla, still trying to recover from Titus' announcement, asked, "What about Livia and Primus? Is Primus staying in the army? Are they going back as well? I know they would help."

"I don't know. I am sure Primus will be faced with the same situation that I faced. Then they will have to decide where they stand and if they go or stay."

The question was quickly answered when Primus and Livia walked in and Primus announced, "I have left the army. I don't fit there any longer."

"You too! What happened?"

"Emericus called for me to report. When I did, he said you were no longer in the army, and he wanted to know where I stood. He asked me if I believed in the gods of Rome and Caesar as a god, or the Jewish God. I told him that I believed in the one true God. He said I must renounce that belief if I was going to stay in the army. I would not do that, so I am out of the army too."

Peter said, "Primus, you have proven the strength of your faith as has Titus. When you give up something you valued for your belief and faith in Jesus, you prove your sincerity. Your relationship with Jesus is not shallow. God notices and will bless both of you.

"But I warn you even though you have experienced trouble already, you can expect trouble again. Jesus never promised a soft easy life. In fact, He said we will have trouble in this life. The evil one promotes troubles for Jesus' followers, but God is stronger. You must stay strong and ask God to see you through whatever trouble you are facing at the time."

Titus responded, "We will try to be prepared. Right now, we need to decide what is the right thing to do and where we should go. Will God help us decide?"

Peter answered, "God has a way of opening and closing doors so you will go in the direction He wants you to go."

Primus looked at Titus and said, "Titus, we have no plans either, so, wherever you are going or whatever you are going to do, Livia and I would like to join you. That is, if you agree."

"Good to hear you say that! We have been together for a long time, Primus. Why should we change now?"

With that the two families circled around Peter. Titus said, "We don't know what the future holds for us. Because of what you have told us, Peter, we are putting our future in the hands of God. I will admit I am nervous about the future. I don't have any control over our future. Yet we are grateful for you bringing the truth about Jesus to us. I believe He will be with us. We will tell others about him."

Peter said, "I can understand your concern about the future, but I assure you that God will be with you every step of the way. The Holy Spirit visited you two days ago and He will go with you to fulfill God's will. I'll pray for you always, and I'll begin right now." Then he asked God to bless these believers, to protect them from the evil one; to provide for them, and fill them with knowledge and wisdom. After Peter finished praying, he said, "Stay strong and rely on the Lord. He will be with you." Then he left for Joppa, and the two families began preparing and packing for their trip to Italia.

Titus told Drusilla he wanted to tell Fishel goodbye. When he found him, Titus thanked him for all he had done. He said, "Fishel, I would not have developed a knowledge and love for Jesus without you. I am indebted to you for that. I encourage you to seek followers of Jesus and learn about Him. All I can offer you for all your help is my gratitude and all of the furnishings we are leaving. Keep them for your family or sell them."

Two days later, there was a ship in the harbor and they hoped passage could be arranged. Titus and Primus located the ship's captain to begin arranging for passage. The captain said he was expecting them, and told them passage had already been arranged and paid for. Emericus had kept his word.

The following morning, both families loaded their belongings onto the ship that would take them back to Naples. After they boarded, they learned there would be another passenger by the name of Pontius Pilate.

Primus asked, "Cornelius, do you think this will cause a problem for us?"

"I doubt it Primus. I was told by the ship's crew Pilate was being sent back to Rome because of charges of misconduct. The legate of Syria has ordered him to appear before Tiberius. He has enough troubles of his own. He will not be interested in us."

XV

Going Home

The voyage back to Naples took one day less than the east bound trip thanks to cooperating winds and good weather. As land came into view, the small group lined up along the rail. Everyone's heart beat a little faster. The appreciation for their homeland was intensified by their long absence. Titus and Primus both wondered what changes might have occurred during their time away. Drusilla wondered how would their new beliefs would be received. They kept looking as the ship followed the coastland toward the port of Naples.

Titus and his family, along with Primus and Livia, disembarked at the fourth hour in the morning. All of their belongings were unloaded and stacked up on the dock by the three men. They had a large pile of things exposed on the dock. Leaving it unguarded would be foolish so Coto stayed with everything while the two families went to seek food and lodging.

Walking on land again was a bigger adjustment for Alexius than the adults, and he was teased about losing his sea legs. But it wasn't long before he was moving faster than the adults. Alexius had grown during the family's time in Judea. Drusilla said, "I don't think it will be long before he is as tall as I am."

After finding an inn where they could eat, they sat down for a meal of familiar Roman cooking. It was then they learned that ten days ago Tiberius died and Caligula was the new Emperor. Titus said, "Didn't Germanicus have a son named, Caligula? And I think there was some connection with Tiberius."

Primus answered, "I don't know. You knew Germanicus better than I." The new Caesar was the subject of conversation until the food was placed before them.

They enjoyed food that they had not had for a long time. Part of it was sent to Coto. After eating, they began discussing their next move, which was finding a place to live. Drusilla was the first to speak, "Does anyone have an idea as to where we should go?"

Titus suggested, "We can go to Aversa where I own a hectare of land. But it would be better if we could locate near some other Jesus believers, and I doubt if there are any believers there."

Primus said, "We could go where I was raised, but I doubt if there are believers there either, and I don't know if we could find houses to live in. It has an old established group of people there that do not accept strangers very well."

Livia said, "That doesn't sound very friendly. In addition to where should we go is the question of whether we should try to stay together."

Titus answered, "I think we should for support and strength. I don't know how our belief in only one God will be accepted."

Drusilla said, "Romans have always been open to more than one god. I don't see how that should be a problem."

Titus responded, "Believing in many gods is not the problem. It is the recognition of Caesar as a god and worshipping him that is the problem. Remember Peter told us there is only one God and that we should worship and honor him only."

"I still don't think that will bother most Romans."

Primus said, "Drusilla, Titus and I left the army because we would not accept Caesar as a god. We don't know how strongly

Caligula will believe he is a god and expect everyone to honor him as a god."

Titus added, "I was even told I could be executed for not worshipping Caesar as a god."

Both Livia and Drusilla were shocked at Titus' statement. Livia said, "I never realized that worshipping Caesar had become so serious. I am surprised that the senate would give their approval of Caesar worship."

Titus said, "I am not sure the Senate was ever consulted, it has been that way ever since I can remember. We need to be cautious about expressing our opinion on the emperors being a god, as well as our worship beliefs."

Primus said, "I agree with Titus. We should not openly talk about our beliefs until we know what people will accept."

Livia asked, "Aren't we supposed to share the salvation message with others?"

Titus answered her, "Yes we are; however, we must be cautious about how we do it. We could be put in confinement or worse. Then we would never have a chance to tell anyone about Jesus. So we should first determine if a person would be open to the message."

Livia said, "I agree."

Drusilla asked, "Where are we going to find people who believe as we do?' No one knew. The conversation came to a halt.

After a lengthy pause, Titus said, "I suggest we go to Aversa. That is the only place that seems available. As I said once before, we can start a vineyard on the hectare of land I have there."

Primus interjected, "One hectare of land will not produce enough grapes to provide for all of us. More land will be needed."

"Maybe we can buy some more land nearby. I have enough money."

Primus said, "I have money too. If we are going to do this together, I need to pay part of the cost."

It was agreed by all to go to Aversa, since no one had any other acceptable suggestion.

Drusilla said, "Titus maybe you and I should go visit my parents and ask them about places to live."

Livia said, "That makes sense, Drusilla. You two go on. Primus, Coto, and I will wait four hours before we start then we will meet you at your father's home. That will give you some time to get re-acquainted with your parents."

Drusilla and Titus started off toward her parents. A brisk walk would get them there in three hours or less. Meanwhile, Livia and Primus rejoined Coto at the seafront. Primus went off to find a donkey and a cart they could use to move their belongings. He found a man with a cart who was willing to move their belongings for a fee. After some negotiations everything was loaded on the man's cart, then they started toward Drusilla's parents.

Drusilla's parents, Lavinia and Robertus were surprised but glad to see their daughter and Titus. Drusilla said, "Mother, Father, here are your grandchildren, Adela and Alexius." Her parents were thrilled at the news that they were grandparents. "We must have a celebration!"

"Fine, father, but first we need to find a house to live in. Actually, we need two houses."

"Two houses? Why do you need two houses?"

"Remember Titus's sister, Livia? She and her husband are with us. Her husband was in the army with Titus, and we have become great friends. They want to live near us, so they need a house too."

"I know of one house; I will try to find another. But tonight, we celebrate my grandchildren. I will invite everybody!"

Just before the celebration started, Livia, Primus, and Coto arrived. Drusilla introduced them to her parents. Her parents received them warmly. Robertus and Lavinia were still glowing from meeting their grandchildren. Primus and Livia relaxed, and everyone felt at ease.

During the celebration, Titus thought it would be a good time to ask about buying additional land since Robertus was in such a good mood. At an opportune time, Titus asked him, "Is there any land for sale around here?"

Robertus asked, "Titus, what do you have in mind to do with the land you want to buy?"

Titus told him, "I want to start a vineyard." Drusilla's father's eyes lit up. "That is a good plan. I own the land around the hectare I gave you, and I will sell you another two hectares. That should give you enough to start."

Night came upon them quickly. Lavinia said, "Why don't all of you stay with us tonight. We can find room for everyone."

"Thank you, Mother, We will."

The next morning, they went to examine the house Robertus knew about. It was close to the land Titus and Primus were buying. Drusilla thought it was acceptable, so she and Titus started moving in. Before the day was over, a second house was found that Livia really liked. Plans were falling into place for the two families. They now had homes and land.

They wasted no time. Grapevine starts were purchased. Titus, Coto, and Primus planted them. They felt God's presence in their labors and each day they all gathered together to pray and recall things Peter had taught them. They discussed the meaning of some of Peter's teaching. Unfortunately, there always seemed to be questions that they were unable to answer.

Titus and Drusilla shared the stories about Jesus and his miracles with Drusilla's parents who liked the stories about the miracles, but they refused to accept the one God only concept or Jesus being God's son.

Robertus said, "Titus, your stories of a god that created the world are ridiculous. The world has always been in existence."

"I used to feel the same way but my view was changed by a man that did miraculous feats."

"Did you talk with this man?"

"No, but I talked with a follower of this man who was an eye-witness to his miracles. He was very convincing. There were others who I talked to that had been affected by this man".

"And this man was Jesus?"

Drusilla joined in, "Yes, father. Mother, can you see what we are talking about?"

Lavinia answered, "You told us this Jesus was crucified. If he was a god, he would never let humans crucify him. No, I don't see what you are talking about. But you can have whatever god you want. What I want now is to hear more about my grandchildren."

Both Drusilla and Titus knew further conversation about Jesus would fall on deaf ears. They would try again at another time.

They discreetly began seeking other believers but found none. They continually expressed goodwill and love to all their neighbors at every opportunity.

The following year there was a financial crisis in Italia. The situation got so bad that many people began having trouble providing food for their families. Primus had used some of their land to raise vegetables for the two families. His efforts were very successful because God had blessed his work. When they saw their neighbors' children stealing produce from their gardens, they started sharing vegetables with those in need.

When people saw the generosity of the two new families, they began to have more respect for them. Another year later, they even began to listen to their testimonies. Soon, some of their neighbors wanted to know more than Titus or any of the others could tell them. Titus said, "I feel like a failure when I cannot answer people's questions. I don't know what to do."

One day at the market while Primus was selling produce, he heard about a man and his wife who openly talked about Jesus. Primus wanted to know where this man and his wife could be found. After getting answers he rushed to Titus' house with Livia. When he told Titus and Drusilla his news, all four got excited and asked, "Who are they? Did you meet them?"

The answer was, "No I did not meet them. I did find out their names are Aquila and Priscilla. They are tentmakers. I was told they had been here but now they were last seen at a market on the south edge of Rome."

Titus said, "We must talk to these people. Do you think they would come here?"

"I don't know, but I would like to talk with them too. It is a four-day journey to Rome, and we all cannot go. By the time we get to Rome and get to the right market, they may have moved to some other location which means we would have to search for them. Making contact might not be easy."

Drusilla said, "Still, someone should go and ask them to come here."

Primus volunteered "What if I went and asked them to come here?"

Titus said, "Primus, I thank you for your offer. You go, and may God bless your efforts."

Four days later, Primus was in Rome asking about believers. The first man he approached responded, "Why would you be interested in them? They are crazy people. They share what everyone else keeps for themselves and refuse to share what everyone else shares."

"What don't they share?"

"Their wives!"

Primus moved on. This was not the right man to talk to. He later discovered that slaves were the best sources of information about Jesus, and they led him to Aquila and Priscilla.

The couple greeted him and asked, "You really came here just to meet us?"

"Not only meet you but to ask you to go back with me and teach my wife and her brother's family more about Jesus."

"Where did you hear about Jesus?"

"From Peter when we were in Judea."

"You have met Peter? If you did, you are indeed blessed."

Primus told them about their background and of their baptism by Peter. He went on to say they had so many questions but nowhere to find answers. "Please go back with me and teach us."

Aquila said, "I am impressed that you traveled for four days and spent two more days to find us in order to learn more about Jesus. How can we refuse you?"

Their return trip took five days because Aquila and Priscilla wanted to tell everyone they met along the way about Jesus. Primus was embarrassed at first, and later began joining in their efforts.

Upon their arrival at Titus and Drusilla's home, Titus thanked them for coming. He immediately wanted to call their neighbors to come to meet them. Drusilla gently said, "Titus, give our guests a chance to rest and to eat something."

Priscilla smiled saying, "Your enthusiasm to learn and share is encouraging. We will not rush away."

Drusilla and Livia prepared a meal. Before they ate, Aquila thanked God for bringing them to people hungry for words about Jesus. During the meal, Aquila asked what they had learned from Peter. All four shared what Peter had told them. What one had forgotten, another would talk about. Then they asked Aquila where they had learned about Jesus.

He said, "We were in Jerusalem during Shavuot (Pentecost) when we heard that a man had been crucified for blasphemy and some of his followers were still making trouble. Then a man we know told us that was not true. He said, 'The man's name was Jesus and he was a prophet from God. The priests would not recognize him because they were jealous of him. They caused his death."

"Yes, Peter told us that as well. Please go on."

"We were about to leave the city when we heard a loud roar of wind. It was so different from anything we had ever heard before. We, like many others investigated. We found eleven men sitting together, each talking in different languages. Strangely, we could hear all of them praising God. At first, we thought it was just some kind of nonsense. But a man in the crowd pointed and said, 'No! That man is talking in my language!' Then another said that one of them was talking in his language.

"There were people in the crowd from at least eleven different countries, and they all heard their native language being spoken. We looked again at these eleven men. They were simple, uneducated men. Everyone in the crowd was perplexed. We knew this was not normal. Something special was taking place. That is when one of the eleven stood up and started to speak. He really had our attention."

Alexius who was listening too, interrupted, "Wow! That must have been some experience. I can't imagine hearing all those different languages at the same time."

"It was unbelievable, Alexius." Then Aquila, turning back to the others, continued, "We learned the speaker was Peter, a follower of Jesus. What Peter said overwhelmed us. First, he said, 'We are not crazy nor are we drunk as some of you think. What is happening is what the prophet Joel said would happen someday. He foretold the day would come when God would pour out his Spirit on people, that men would see visions, and people would prophesy. God is among us right now! That is why we are able to speak in languages we do not know." He paused, allowing the people time to consider what he said. Everyone was listening very intently.

Priscilla finished their account. "Then Peter continued, 'Listen to what I am about to tell you. God performed miracles and wonderful things through Jesus, whom you put to death by nailing him to a cross. He died and was placed in a tomb near Golgotha. But God raised him from the dead because death could not hold him. He is the one King David said would not be held in a grave, the one who would be resurrected. I tell you this man, Jesus, that you killed, is alive today! God resurrected him. We eleven are eyewitnesses to this. Now he has ascended into heaven and is sitting at the right hand of God. His Holy Spirit is what you are seeing and hearing right now. So be assured of this: God has made Jesus, whom you crucified, both Lord and Savior.'"

Priscilla took a drink and continued, "The crowd was stunned by Peter's proclamation. Some were crying. Everyone felt guilty; we did as well, and we had not even been in Jerusalem when it happened. Someone in the crowd asked Peter, 'What can we do?' Peter answered, 'Repent and be baptized, every one of you, in the name of Jesus Christ for the forgiveness of your sins. Then you will receive the gift of the Holy Spirit.'

"Three thousand people responded and were baptized. All eleven men were performing the baptisms and praying for each person. They were still baptizing people when the sun set. We watched until it was too dark to see. Then we went to find a place to stay the night. All night long my heart drew me to what Peter had said. The next morning Priscilla and I sought Peter and were baptized. We stayed and listened to Peter and the other eyewitnesses for a month."

Livia said, "There are times when I feel I have sinned against God because of something I did. Do I need to be baptized again?"

Aquila said, "No, remember when you were baptized, you received the Holy Spirit, and you also were covered by God's grace at that time."

"What do you mean by covered by God's grace? I never understood about grace."

Priscilla answered, "When Jesus died, His blood substituted for our sins that require eternal death if they are not forgiven. That made us eligible to live with God forever. That is grace. However, there is a little more to it. God is merciful; he knows we humans are weak and that we would be tempted by evil thoughts that could lead us away from him. So, he provides forgiveness when we fall short of his standards. We are recipients of his unmerited favor. But do not take this gift lightly. If you continue to do the same sin over and over, then you fall under God's judgment. Just remember that when you are tempted, God will provide a way to escape the temptation. His Holy Spirit will live in the heart of Believers and give them the power to say 'no' to the temptation. But each one must decide to follow it."

Drusilla said, "Sometimes it seems difficult to follow Jesus. I try but I do not know if I am or not. I fear I do not know enough."

Aquila in a reassuring manner said, "Do not try to make it difficult. Following Jesus can be as simple as remembering what he said when asked what was the most important commandment. He answered, 'Love your God with all your heart, and love others as you love yourself.' If your heart is full of love for God, there will be no room for anything else. Follow what your heart tells you. It will tell you whether something is right or wrong."

Drusilla said, "I remember Peter telling us the same thing."

Titus said, "We must invite our neighbors in to hear what is being said."

Primus added, "Yes, we should. There is much to hear." They invited many people who came to Titus' house every day for a week. Aquila and Priscilla talked until their voices gave out. Ten people were baptized. Aquila informed Titus at end of the week that they needed to return to Rome. We need to check on our tent making business.

Drusilla said, "We wish you could stay but we understand. You have been so helpful, and you have given us much encouragement."

The baptized believers came to say goodbye. Before they left, Aquila said to all, "At this time Caesar has not pressured the Jews to abide by his law to worship him as a god, but he still expects all Roman citizens to do so. You who are Romans be cautious about those with whom you share your beliefs. You who are Jewish, Caesar is changing. He is becoming more paranoid and tyrannical. He even appointed his horse as a consul. The situation for you could change so be cautious. I will pray for your well-being and growth in the Lord."

Titus asked Aquila, "Will you come back?"

"We go where God leads us, so I cannot say if we will be back."

"Will we ever see you again?"

"I'm certain you will, if not in this world, then in God's kingdom."

Everyone came together around Aquila and Priscilla and thanked God for their visit and teaching they had provided. They asked God to grant them safe travels and protection from the dark powers of the evil one.

As the couple left, Titus and Drusilla offered personal thanks for their coming and teaching. They felt they had found two especially strong friends to go with their new friends who had accepted Jesus.

XVI

An Unshakeable Belief

Primus and Livia came by two days later. "We feel lost without Aquila and Priscilla to talk with. They were great encouragers."

Titus said, "We must not feel that way. We must believe that God will direct us, if we will listen for his voice."

Livia said, "I feel better when the four of us are all together. It is when I am alone that I am weak."

Titus thought for a moment, then said, "Why don't we set aside one day a week to come together and pray and talk about God?"

"That is a good idea. We can invite the new believers to join us."

Drusilla said, "If God is to be first in our hearts. Let's make the first day of the week our day to pray and praise God." The others thought that was a great suggestion.

The next Sunday Primus, Livia, those who had been baptized and two new couples joined together with Titus, Drusilla, and Coto. They prayed and praised God. They discussed many of the things Aquila and Priscilla had taught. When the sun was at its highest point in the sky, Alexius and Adela interrupted.

"Mother, we are hungry! Are we going to eat anything?"

Drusilla asked, "Does anyone object if we stop for a little while?"

Primus said, "I doubt if God would object if we stopped to eat something. It will provide an opportunity to thank him for our blessings."

A pattern was established. Each Sunday there would be a period of prayer and praise, then food and fellowship followed by discussions about God and Jesus.

Drusilla said to Titus, "I want to talk to my parents again. I know they do not have very much longer to live, and they need God's salvation."

Titus said, "I'll go with you. Maybe I can help."

"No, I feel it would be better if I went alone."

Robertus and Lavinia welcomed their daughter and asked her why she did not bring their grandchildren. She said, "I wanted to talk to you about eternity."

Her mother responded, "Oh my, what a subject! Drusilla, there is no eternity. When you die, you're dead. There is nothing more."

"Mother, there is life after you die here. The question is where will you spend it."

Her father said, "Drusilla, didn't you hear your mother? When you die, you're dead. This talk about another life is nonsense."

"Father hear me out, please."

"I know you just want to talk about this Jesus and the god you are telling people about."

"Yes! I do."

"We and everyone in this area have heard about the gatherings and what you and Titus are telling people. Well, we don't want to hear any more about it, and I advise you to forget about this Jesus before you get in trouble. You don't seem to realize the danger you could face."

"I do realize the authorities are not in agreement with what we say, but I can't forget about Jesus and you would not either if you knew Him like I do."

Robertus was becoming impatient, "If this is all you want to talk about, then go. Come back when you realize your wrongful ways."

"Mother will you hear me?"

"I agree with your father. You must forget all this nonsense."

"I'll go. I am sorry you feel this way. I will pray God will soften your hearts."

Drusilla was very sad because her parents would not accept Jesus. Yet she continued to share with others at every opportunity. More people started coming to Titus' house on Sundays until there were more people than they could comfortably handle. Livia suggested she and Primus could open their home as well. So, a second group of believers was established.

Before long more people were baptized and joined the believers, hence; a third group of believers was started. One of the couples said they had a large room and would begin hosting believers on Sundays. Titus, Drusilla and Primus and Livia still met together, along with the leaders of the third group. They would encourage one another and discuss what to do on Sundays. They also shared information about anyone who was in need of food or had problems. Someone would go to the aid of that person when there was a need.

Every Sunday the believers would gather together in one of the three groups, to worship and have fellowship. Before another year passed a fourth group was established. Titus praised God for the growth. Everything was going well; the message of salvation was spreading.

Then a believer in Titus's group warned him. "Titus, our magistrate has learned of our meetings and is asking questions. I am fearful that something may happen because I have heard that Emperor Caligula has been having delusions of divinity. He wants everybody to recognize him as a god and worship him. Even the Jews are required to do so."

Titus reassured him, "Do not be afraid. Caligula has felt he is a god from the first day he became Emperor. But our God is in control. We just don't know what his plans might be. Rely on your faith, God will be with us no matter what might happen. Peter once told me, 'Faith that costs you nothing is a very shallow faith'. Even if we are arrested and put to death because of our beliefs, we must stay strong. The Holy Spirit will be with us. By doing so, we prove our faith in Jesus and death just puts us with the Lord sooner, where we will be forever."

"Maybe so, but what about my wife and children if I am taken? I could no longer protect or provide for them if I were arrested."

Others began to get nervous because someone from the magistrate's office was questioning people. Each Sunday several people asked what should they do?

Titus spoke to those who were worshiping at his home, "Have faith my friends. It appears that we will be tested soon. If you are arrested, God will be with your family and He will care for them. As for death, we all know that at some point each of us will stop breathing but our existence in heaven will last forever." He delivered the same message to the other three groups.

On the next Sunday, again, Titus tried to strengthen and encourage the believers. He prayed for the Holy Spirit's help and protection. His last remarks were, "Remember God knows what is happening, and He is in control. Even if events are not what we want, or even if things become dangerous, keep remembering, our destiny is with Jesus and what happens in eternity is what is important."

A few weeks later, a stranger came to Titus' house on Sunday. He was welcomed by all the believers, but he said nothing until Titus started talking about Jesus. The man stood up, "Stop all of this foolish talk! You should be praising Caesar Caligula, not someone I have never heard of."

Titus listened to the stranger's ranting. When he stopped, Titus tried to calm the stranger. He said, "Since you have not heard about Jesus, let me tell you who he is and what he has done for all of us, you included."

"I'm not interested. You should not be telling people this nonsense. You are just causing trouble. You must explain yourself tomorrow morning to the magistrate." With that he left.

Everyone was in shock. Some of the believers left. Those who stayed, were asking each other, "What does this mean?" Within hours Titus received a formal order to appear before the magistrate the next morning.

Drusilla said, "We need to pray continually until Titus comes home from the magistrate." Those who were still there began saying prayers and continued for a period of time. As darkness approached, everyone left for their homes. As they left, Drusilla reminded everyone to continue praying and especially to pray tomorrow for Titus."

Titus said to Alexius, "Go to Primus and Livia and tell them what happened here. Tell them I suggest they leave their home and go someplace else. They should even consider moving permanently."

Alexius looked at his father and asked, "Is it really that serious?"

"Yes, it is. Alexius, I don't know what is going to happen, but whatever does happen just remember I love you, your mother and sister very much. If anything happens to me, take care of your mother and sister. Always rely on God."

"I will, father." With that 15-year-old Alexius left to deliver his message.

When Primus heard the message, rather than leave, he and Livia went back with Alexius, to be with Titus and Drusilla. No one slept that night. They prayed for God's intervention and for the strength to face whatever happened.

Morning came sooner than anyone wanted. Primus insisted on going with Titus to see the magistrate, even though Titus told him not to go. "I am going to support you, so don't try to stop me." Then they all prayed. Titus prayed, "God, you have been faithful in directing us and now I ask that you give us the strength to face whatever we must face in order for our will to be done." After telling Drusilla how he loved her and that he wanted God's will to be done, Titus and Primus left. Alexius spoke out, "I will take care of mother and Adela". Livia wrapped her arms around Drusilla and Adela.

Titus was ordered to stand before the magistrate, while Primus was ordered to the back of the room and told not to speak. The magistrate started, "Cornelius, I am told you are talking about some Jew who is dead and that He is the son of the true God. And you are encouraging people to worship him and not Caesar. Is this true?"

Titus answered, "I served 25 years in the Roman army. I took an oath to obey Caesar. I have never been disloyal to this Caesar or any other. However, the way you ask it, I have no choice but to answer, yes. But there is so much more involved in what you ask. For instance, this Jew is named Jesus and he is not dead. He was raised from the grave and is in God's kingdom. Would you let me tell you about him?"

"That will not be necessary. Just answer my questions. Do you praise Caesar Caligula as well as this Jew?"

"Sir, I have always supported all Caesars and have never spoken against any of them."

"That is not what I asked; do you praise Caligula and recognize him as a god?"

"Sir, Caligula is an Emperor. He is not a god. There is only one God, the creator of this world."

"Not recognizing Caligula as a god and not paying him homage is a capital offense. You should know this. If you persist in your line of thinking you will condemn yourself."

"I will obey all laws and support Caligula, but I will not worship him as a god."

"Do you realize you have just condemned yourself? You face an execution."

"Then as a Roman citizen I appeal to the Centuriate Assembly."

"You have that right. You will be imprisoned until they agree to hear your case. Guards, take him away."

Primus heard all that was said. He had not been allowed to speak but was allowed to leave. He went straight to Drusilla. "Titus was arrested and faces a death charge. He has appealed. He will face the Centuriate Assembly. He is to be held until his case is heard. Then he will be sent to Rome for trial. You and your children must leave. As soon as the authorities find out you are Titus' wife, they will come for you. Come home with me until we can find a safe place for you to go."

Drusilla objected, "No! I want to go to Titus."

"Drusilla, it is too dangerous; you would be arrested as well. You must think of your children as well as Titus. It is important that you carry on the work Titus and you were doing. God will be with Titus."

As the tears streamed down her cheeks, she told the children to get together whatever they could carry. Blinded by the tears in her eyes, Drusilla packed a few things which she gave to Coto, who had been listening to all that was happening. He, said, "I will go to be with Titus." Primus intervened, "Coto, I know of your loyalty but you will be needed to protect and help Drusilla and her children. Reluctantly he agreed.

Drusilla said to her female slave, who had been with her since childhood, "You are free. Go wherever you want."

"I have spent most of my life serving you. There is no reason for me to walk away now, I want to go with you."

"All right, come with us." Then she took Adela in one hand and with the other, she reached for Alexius' arm. "Alexius, I will look to you as my protector."

"Mother, as God is my witness, I will care for you as long as you live." It was then she noticed that Alexius had taken his father's sword. Drusilla had not seen it since Titus left the army. She was surprised Alexius had thought about taking it. She said nothing to him. Following Primus, they walked away without looking back.

Drusilla's parents heard of Titus being arrested. They were worried about Drusilla and the children. Robertus decided to go to Titus and try to talk some sense into him. He discovered where Titus was being held, and he went there hoping he could see him. He was allowed to enter the compound to look for Titus. When he found Titus he asked, "What were you thinking when you were before the magistrate?"

Titus answered. "I was thinking about how to tell the magistrate about Jesus."

Robertus threw up his hands, "Titus, all you have to do, is say you recognize that Claudius is a god. You can keep this other God as well."

"Robertus, it is not that simple. If I said that Claudius is a god, I am putting him on the same level as the true God and that is not acceptable to the God, I believe in."

"Titus, Titus! Don't you realize you will be killed? And if that doesn't frighten you, think of the danger you are putting Drusilla and your children in."

"I know exactly the situation I am in and what I face, but I will not go against what I believe."

Robertus could not understand how Titus could be so stubborn in his thinking. He asked, "Don't you love Drusilla and your children?"

"Of course, I do; never doubt that I love my family.

"What about your land? Do you realize you could lose your land and home? Or at the very least you will leave your family without a place to live? You are even endangering their lives; they could be killed as well as you. Is that what you want?"

"I know what you say is true, but I trust my God to be with my family. Whatever He wants to happen, will happen regardless of what I say or do. I believe God will provide and protect them."

"Your God is no different than any other and will do nothing. Titus you are a fool. I came here in hopes of saving my daughter and grandchildren, but I see you will be of no help." Robertus left.

A month later, Titus was taken to Rome where he went before the Centuriate Assembly, which included Caligula. He was asked, "Is it true that you refuse to pay homage to Caligula as a god?"

Titus answered, "It is not that I refused. It is that I believe there is only one God, and I praise him only. He came to this world as a man named Jesus and was crucified for mankind's sins. He was buried but God resurrected him and he is alive today."

The Senator in charge of hearing Titus's case replied, "What you say is a child's story. Recant and praise Caligula as a god. Then you may go free."

"I have never said anything against Caligula. I have served in the army protecting Rome's interests for more than twenty years. Many will testify to my loyalty to Rome. But I cannot say that Caligula is a god. There is only the one true God and I will praise him only."

Caligula was furious. He screamed, "Kill him now! Right where he stands! Kill him; I will not tolerate this attitude." Titus was surprised at the outburst.

"Cornelius, do you have any more to say?"

"If I may, let me tell you about Jesus. He is a loving God who wants to save you."

"Silence! We are not going to waste our time on stories. This is your last chance. Will you worship Caligula as god?"

"No."

"In that case, you have condemned yourself. Guards, take him out and kill him. Then confiscate his property and kill his family. This type of thinking must be rooted out and destroyed."

Under guard, Titus left the room praising God. As the guards led him outside to an open area Titus said, "Thank you, Jesus, for being part of my life while I walked this land. You are a glorious God!"

Suddenly, his eyes brightened, a smile came on his face "I see big golden gates in the clouds opening, and someone is walking out toward me. Oh, my, it is Jesus! I am finally going to meet Jesus, face to face!"

Those were his last words. His body collapsed to the ground. At that moment many stadia away, Drusilla winced from a pain in her heart. She knew God was telling her Titus was with Him now. She thanked God for making Titus death occur quickly.

Coto, Drusilla and her children went to Primus' house on the day of Titus' confinement. They stayed only one night. When morning came, all of them left the area. They traveled all day to get as far away as possible. When they stopped for the evening, Primus said to Drusilla, "I think we should separate. Coto can go with you for your protection. We will be two different voices to spread God's message over a wider area. I think Titus would approve."

Drusilla agreed and said, "I will speak in honor of Titus, and tell of his faith. I think he would want that." With words of encouragement and praying for God's direction, the two families separated. Livia and Primus went north and Coto, Drusilla and her two children went east.

With the assistance of other believers, Drusilla and her children moved from one group of believers to another for almost a year. As they met and worshiped with believers everywhere, they were would be invited to speak. Their testimony related to their time with Peter and their acceptance of Jesus Christ. They ended their talk by telling of Titus resigning from the army because of his strong faith in God and that he maintained his faith until he was killed.

Their powerful witness and telling of Titus' unshakeable belief, not only encouraged believers throughout Italia, it inspired and strengthened all who listened. Their speaking drew the attention of the authorities, who were becoming more and more aggressive toward the followers of Jesus. Magistrates eager to please Caligula began sending spies into groups thought to be believers.

Any individuals identified as believers were arrested, and most of the time, never heard from again. There were reports of horrible deaths of believers in Rome that were passed from one group of believers to another. Yet, people saw something different in the lives of believers, and they wanted what they saw. They still were accepting Christ and being baptized even though there was a fear of arrest and possible death. People truly believed there was something more than present daily life.

Drusilla told Coto he should go separately and give his testimony to as many as possible. The decision to do so was difficult for him because he felt it would leave Drusilla unprotected. She reminded him that God was her protector and His will should be accepted. Coto reluctantly agreed and left.

Primus and Livia were instrumental as well in spreading the message of Jesus Christ until spies reported them. News of Primus and Livia's arrest reached Drusilla. She immediately began praying for their protection, if it was God's will. If that was not God's will, she prayed He would allow their departure to be easy and quick. While she was still praying, two men arrived at the home where she was staying. Alexius heard them asking the owners if they knew where Drusilla was staying. He unsheathed his father's sword and stood ready to defend his mother. Drusilla put her hand on his arm and quietly said, "No! that is not the way. We will ask God to protect us. Just be still."

The owner was successful in persuading the two men to leave without conducting a search. After being told they were safe, Alexius said to Drusilla, "Mother, I believe in Jesus the same as you, but I told father I would protect you and Adela. I intend to keep my word."

"Alexius, keeping your word is a good thing but learning to trust God is better."

"I do trust the Lord, mother but I want to always be ready if His will is to use me."

Drusilla continued witnessing to people in different locations. Finally, it was too dangerous for her to remain in Italia, so with help from some believers, Drusilla and her two children escaped from Italia and went to Corinth.

Coto remained in Italia and spoke boldly about Jesus until he was arrested and put to death.

First Century Glossary

Actarius – Military clerk
Armicustos – Supplier of weapons
Castrum – Army camp
Centuria – Division of the army, 80 to 100 men
  (**plural** – centuriae)
Centurion – Officer in charge of a centuria
  (**plural** – centurions)
Cohort – Division of the army, 6 centuriae
Contubernium – Division of the army, 8 miles (soldiers)
  (**plural** – Contubernias)
Decanus – Leader of a contubernium
  (**plural** – decani)
Denarius – unit of Roman money (equal to a day's wages)
Domus – home of wealthy person/ large & spacious
Imperator – supreme officer of the army
Insulae – home of poor person/ cramped & fire prone
Legate – commander of an army
Legionary – member of heavy infantry
  (**plural** – legionaries)
Miles – common foot soldier
Optio – second in command of a centuria
  (**plural** – optiones)
Palla – woman's garment worn over the head & shoulders
Pilus Prior – senior centurion in a cohort, in charge of the cohort
Sasterces – unit of Roman money
Schoenus – Roman unit of distance
Signiful – standard bearer of a centuria

Stadium – approx. 609 feet; 8 ½ stadia = 1 mile
    (plural – stadia)
Stola – woman's garment similar to a long dress
Tirone – basic trainee
Tribune – Commander of a legion

List of characters

Adela – Titus Cornelius' daughter
Alexius – Titus Cornelius' son
Aquila – Male Christian who taught others
Arbelardus – Tribune of the legion in Italy
Augustus Caesar – Roman Emperor 63BC to 14 AD
Breanus – basic training instructor
Caligula – Roman Emperor from 37AD to 41AD
Coto – Titus Cornelius' slave
Drusilla – Titus Cornelius' wife
Emericus – senior centurion in Titus' cohort
Fidelis – Titus Cornelius' father
Fishel – Hebrew man
Germanicus – commander in chief of Roman army
Jesus – the Son of God
Lavinia – Titus Cornelius' mother-in-law
Livia – Titus Cornelius' sister
Ludo – centurion in Capernaum
Marcus – centurion of the third centuria
Peter – an apostle of Christianity
Pontius Pilate – Roman governor of Judea
Primus Constant – friend & fellow soldier of Titus
Quintus Crassus – Roman Senator & Cornelius' owner
Priscilla – wife of Aquila and a teacher
Robertus – Titus Cornelius' father-in-law
Titus Cornelius –Roman centurion
Tiberius – Roman Emperor from 14AD to 37AD

The historical account as recorded by Luke, in the first century.

Acts, chapter 10

1At Caesarea there was a man named Cornelius, a centurion in what was known as the Italian Regiment. 2He and all his family were devout and God-fearing; he gave generously to those in need and prayed to God regularly. 3One day at about three in the afternoon he had a vision. He distinctly saw an angel of God, who came to him and said, "Cornelius!"

4Cornelius stared at him in fear. "What is it, Lord?" he asked.

The angel answered, "Your prayers and gifts to the poor have come up as a memorial offering before God. 5Now send men to Joppa to bring back a man named Simon who is called Peter. 6He is staying with Simon the tanner, whose house is by the sea."

7When the angel who spoke to him had gone, Cornelius called two of his servants and a devout soldier who was one of his attendants. 8He told them everything that had happened and sent them to Joppa.

Peter's Vision

9About noon the following day as they were on their journey and approaching the city, Peter went up on the roof to pray. 10He became hungry and wanted something to eat, and while the meal was being prepared, he fell into a trance. 11He saw heaven opened and something like a large sheet being let down to earth by its four corners. 12It contained all kinds of four-footed animals, as well as reptiles and birds. 13Then a voice told him, "Get up, Peter. Kill and eat."

14"Surely not, Lord!" Peter replied. "I have never eaten anything impure or unclean."

15The voice spoke to him a second time, "Do not call anything impure that God has made clean."

16This happened three times, and immediately the sheet was taken back to heaven.

17While Peter was wondering about the meaning of the vision, the men sent by Cornelius found out where Simon's house was and stopped at the gate. 18They called out, asking if Simon who was known as Peter was staying there.

19While Peter was still thinking about the vision, the Spirit said to him, "Simon, three men are looking for you. 20So get up and go downstairs. Do not hesitate to go with them, for I have sent them."

21Peter went down and said to the men, "I'm the one you're looking for. Why have you come?"

22The men replied, "We have come from Cornelius the centurion. He is a righteous and God-fearing man, who is respected by all the Jewish people. A holy angel told him to ask you to come to his house so that he could hear what you have to say." 23Then Peter invited the men into the house to be his guests.

Peter at Cornelius's House

The next day Peter started out with them, and some of the believers from Joppa went along. 24The following day he arrived in Caesarea. Cornelius was expecting them and had called together his relatives and close friends. 25As Peter entered the house, Cornelius met him and fell at his feet in reverence. 26But Peter made him get up. "Stand up," he said, "I am only a man myself."

27While talking with him, Peter went inside and found a large gathering of people. 28He said to them: "You are well aware that it is against our law for a Jew to associate with or visit a Gentile. But God has shown me that I should not call anyone impure or unclean. 29So when I was sent for, I came without raising any objection. May I ask why you sent for me?"

30Cornelius answered: "Three days ago I was in my house praying at this hour, at three in the afternoon. Suddenly a man in shining clothes stood before me 31and said, 'Cornelius, God has heard your prayer and remembered your gifts to the poor. 32Send to Joppa for Simon who is called Peter. He is a guest in the home of Simon the tanner, who lives by the sea.' 33So I sent for you immediately, and it was good of you to come. Now we are all here in the presence of God to listen to everything the Lord has commanded you to tell us."

34Then Peter began to speak: "I now realize how true it is that God does not show favoritism 35but accepts from every nation the one who fears him and does what is right. 36You know the message God sent to the people of Israel, announcing the good news of peace through Jesus Christ, who is Lord of all. 37You know what has happened throughout the province of Judea, beginning in Galilee after the baptism that John preached— 38how God anointed Jesus of Nazareth with the Holy Spirit and power, and how he went around doing good and healing all who were under the power of the devil, because God was with him.

39"We are witnesses of everything he did in the country of the Jews and in Jerusalem. They killed him by hanging him on a cross, 40but God raised him from the dead on the third day and caused him to be seen. 41He was not seen by all the people, but by witnesses whom God had already chosen—by us who ate and drank with him after he rose from the dead. 42 He commanded us to preach to the people and to testify that he is the one whom God appointed as judge of the living and the dead. 43 All the prophets testify about him that everyone who believes in him receives forgiveness of sins through his name."

44While Peter was still speaking these words, the Holy Spirit came on all who heard the message. 45The circumcised believers who had come with Peter were astonished that the gift of the Holy Spirit had been poured out even on Gentiles. 46For they heard them speaking in tongues and praising God.

Then Peter said, 47"Surely no one can stand in the way of their being baptized with water. They have received the Holy Spirit just as we have." 48So he ordered that they be baptized in the name of Jesus Christ. Then they asked Peter to stay with them for a few days.

New International Version

CPSIA information can be obtained
at www.ICGtesting.com
Printed in the USA
BVHW042048170222
629409BV00003B/22